THE BOOK OF THE CRIME

THE BOOK OF
THE CRIME

Elizabeth Daly

FELONY & MAYHEM PRESS • NEW YORK

All the characters and events portrayed in this work are fictitious.

THE BOOK OF THE CRIME

A Felony & Mayhem mystery

PRINTING HISTORY
First edition (Rinehart): 1951
Felony & Mayhem edition: 2016

ISBN: 978-1-63194-093-4

Manufactured in the United States of America

Library of Congress Cataloging-in-Publication Data

Names: Daly, Elizabeth, 1878-1967 author.
Title: The book of the crime / Elizabeth Daly.
Description: Felony & Mayhem edition. | New York : Felony & Mayhem
Press,
[2016]
Identifiers: LCCN 2016029599 | ISBN 9781631940934
Subjects: LCSH: Gamadge, Henry (Fictitious character)--Fiction. |
GSAFD:
Mystery fiction.
Classification: LCC PS3507.A4674 B65 2016 | DDC 813/.54--dc23
LC record available at https://lccn.loc.gov/2016029599

CONTENTS

The icon above says you're holding a copy of a book in the Felony & Mayhem "Vintage" category. These books were originally published prior to about 1965, and feature the kind of twisty, ingenious puzzles beloved by fans of Agatha Christie and John Dickson Carr. If you enjoy this book, you may well like other "Vintage" titles from Felony & Mayhem Press.

For more about these books, and other Felony & Mayhem titles, or to place an order, please visit our website at:

www.FelonyAndMayhem.com

Other "Vintage" titles from

FELONY&MAYHEM

THE BOOK OF THE CRIME

CHAPTER ONE

Dog Walkers

A GIRL AND A DOG came down the steep brownstone steps; the dog in short, frog-like leaps (he was a Boston terrier, large for his breed), the girl holding on to his leash with one hand, to her cap-like hat with the other. It was a dark, cold April day, six o'clock in the afternoon, and she pulled her fur coat around her when they reached the sidewalk.

She would have turned left to Madison, but the dog preferred the long stretch to Fifth—the Austen house was near the Madison Avenue corner. She followed, indifferent. Rena Austen did not care for the dog Aby, he was the only dog in her life that she had never liked: his brindled coat always felt hot and damp to the hand, his hindquarters hung loose on him and waggled disagreeably at a gesture or a word. He was a sycophant and a coward. But she realized that she ought to feel

1

grateful to Aby, since he was her excuse for getting out of the house and away from human company at this depressing hour. By human company she meant that of the Austens; she seldom saw anybody else.

That narrow house! Squeezed between two others like it, with only a sliver of front showing, but so much of it extending back and back to the limits of the lot. Just a sliver of yard beside the kitchen, and Aby wasn't allowed *there*. The cook would soon have him out of it with a broom.

Dark narrow rooms, dark stairs, dark corners. A perfect trap to her eyes, but plenty of space for a family of four, and too much, she would have thought, for the old gentleman who had lived there and had willed it to Gray Austen, her husband. But the old gentleman had had a family once, she supposed. Now she and Gray had the second-floor back suite; Gray's brother and sister, Jerome and Hildreth, had the third floor; the servants were above. Just right for comfort.

What was wrong with them?

Aby, as usual, kept her waiting on the Fifth Avenue corner in the chill wind, while she looked at the letter box and thought that she had nobody to write to. The only friend she had had in New York, the only one to whom she could possibly write an intimate letter, was married and abroad. And even if there was anybody to write to, what could she say? It would sound well, the kind of thing she had in mind! It would be a nice thing to tell anyone. "My husband was an airman, he will always be lame from a war wound, he walks with a brace. I met him on a bench in Central Park, while I still had that good job you got me; I fell in love with him, and we were married in a month. That was about a year ago. He had plenty of money, because his uncle left him an income for life, and an old house here; he and his brother and sister came on from Oregon to live here, after the war. I have everything, and I had nothing and nobody. I wasn't a child, I was nineteen years old—it was a love match.

"And in three weeks—three weeks!—I decided that we had both made a fearful mistake."

Aby consented to be dragged away from the lamppost, and trotted ahead of her along the avenue, snuffling.

Seven weeks, thought Rena. People didn't behave like that—fall in and out of love in seven weeks. Gray said they didn't, and denied it so far as he was concerned—absolutely denied it. He wouldn't let her even mention it. But he had made the mistake too, whatever he said; she must have been as deceptive unconsciously as he had been—that melancholy, beautiful young man with his braced leg; his dark eyes had looked so kind. But he was far from kind, and his moods were so black that sometimes she felt afraid of him.

It was vulgar to tire of a marriage in a year. What could anybody think, but that she had married for what she could get out of it, the alimony? And a lame man, a war hero too. It was out of the question.

The registrar had been so nice; it had really been very solemn. Rena had meant never to leave Gray Austen, and perhaps "for better, for worse" meant that people must get over their whims and stand by their bargain, and not try to get out of it on the excuse that they hadn't understood what they were letting themselves in for. Rena's whim had lasted a year. "Oh, if it were not for Aby," she thought, as they turned east at the corner, "I needn't go back into that house again. But I could shove him inside when Norah opened the door, and just turn around and go."

Go where? Live on what, until she got another job—if she ever did? "I know Gray would never let me have a divorce, and what respectable person would help me to get one?"

Was it their idleness that made the Austen family so tiresome? None of them did anything. Jerome and Hildreth lived on Gray, Gray lived on his income. There was an excuse for him, and he'd gone into the war so young that he'd never had any other kind of work at all. But Jerome had been an accountant in Portland, Hildreth had had a position outside Portland as a librarian. Hildreth, the eldest of them, wasn't more than forty; but not one of them seemed to have the slightest intention of doing anything again for the rest of their lives. Hildreth pretended to run the house, but they had inherited all of old Mr. Austen's servants, and *they* ran the house—Hildreth didn't spend an hour a day on it. Jerome lolled about, ate and drank, amused himself.

The others of course could fill up their time as Gray couldn't—they got around, picked up friends, went to plays and concerts and exhibitions, travelled; flitted back and forth between New York and Portland to settle the family affairs. They'd just come home from that last trip. But Gray—wouldn't any other normal human being find himself something to do? He didn't suffer at all, he was an intelligent, well-read man. Well, that brought it all back to the original trouble and question—Gray's case. He was simply one of those cases, she supposed, and his problem wasn't that he couldn't dance or play golf or tennis, lead an active life; it came from the effects of the war itself on him, and his recovery would be difficult and slow. She was there presumably to help him; and all she could think of was getting away.

At first she had wondered whether his first wife's death had been what he couldn't recover from; but after he told her about it, before they were married and indeed almost as soon as they began to talk at all intimately, he had not referred to it again. Nobody talked about the first wife, and why should they, to her? A sad subject—Gray had married her here, very soon after he got his discharge and came to New York early in 1946. They were married two years, and then she had died of virulent pneumonia, there in the Austen house. Gray had stood his loneliness for a year, and then he had met Rena in the park.

Two years! The first Mrs. Gray Austen had lasted two years, and the second Mrs. Austen didn't look like lasting for more than one. Had the other girl been so worn down by boredom and hopelessness and strain that she couldn't put up any resistance to the disease? Such a nice little thing she had sounded like, a hostess in a restaurant: Gray couldn't exactly be accused of fortune-hunting! Pretty, with Rena's light colouring, and as isolated in the world as Rena was.

The wretched Aby tried to stop at the Madison Avenue corner, but Rena wouldn't let him; mean of her, she thought, but he was such a dawdler. A big dog on a short leash was coming along the street, paying no attention to them, but Aby got behind her. "He can't help it," she thought, feeling angry because the man with the other dog laughed at Aby and at her. The big dog ignored the whole thing. Traffic streamed or jolted past them, cabs and buses taking people home. Huge trucks ground by, horns blew. Not many pedestrians, though, at this hour with the stores closed. Just dog walkers, in hot weather or cold, rain or shine.

She had followed the old track again, the course of the sign that stood for infinity; around first one loop and then the other, back to where the lines crossed: the walk with Aby always just got her back to where the lines crossed. Here they were near the last corner, and then there would be the big apartment house to pass, and a house, and then the Austen house. Would they all be in the library waiting for cocktails as usual? Or would they be down in the front basement, knocking balls around on the old pool table—mixing the cocktails themselves at the bar? The liquor was all down there, and so Gray was down there often. Not that he exactly *drank*, Rena protested to herself; at least he carried it all right, but it seemed to make people short-tempered instead of gay. In the long run, of course.

She and Aby were passing the service alley of the apartment house now, and Aby was always interested in garbage cans. She let him stop a minute to fuss and sniff there in his unattractive fervent way, with her eye out for superintendents and porters; but they never seemed to be around at that hour. Suddenly he glanced over his shoulder, started violently, and disappeared behind one of the cans; Rena almost lost her grip on his leash. A voice said: "I just wanted to apologize."

She looked around and up; the big dog's owner was big too, big and tall, with a tweed overcoat hanging open and a soft hat in his hand. The wolfhound's leash was wrapped around the other hand, and his collar gripped firmly in gloved fingers.

"Gawain wouldn't hurt a fly," said the hound's owner.

"I notice you have him pretty tight," said Rena, responding to the man's smile with one of her own.

"Well, he might nose up a little. Leave your pup where he is a minute, if he likes it there; I wanted to explain—I didn't laugh to be rude or anything."

"I know Aby's funny, but he can't help it."

The big man was youngish, and his face had a skin-grafting job all the way down his left cheek. He had tawny hair; he looked at her from lively blue eyes, half-closed.

"That's his name, is it? I know him from before the war," said the big man. "What I wanted to explain. He's getting on, poor old guy. Many a time I used to meet old Mr. Austen walking him, when I was walking the pup we had then—police dog it was. Old Mr. Austen and I had many a good laugh over this Aby. So today I—didn't mean to be rude."

"Perfectly all right," said Rena. "I suppose I'm a little touchy about him."

"Don't blame you. The best dog we ever had—best pedigree, I mean—he wasn't quite right in the head. Bull terrier, and up in the country he used to come home otherwise all right, but with the tip of his tail pretty nearly bit off."

Rena hadn't heard herself laugh for so long that she startled herself now.

"My name's Ordway," said the young man. He jerked his head backwards: "We live across the street there. Always lived there, since this region was built up—I mean the family has. Austens too. I understand there are Austens there again."

"Yes, I'm Mrs. Austen."

"Oh. Yes." He glanced at her briefly. "He caught it worse than some of us. I've seen him out walking the pup. I suppose that's your husband."

"Yes, Gray."

"Well…" Conversation halted. Then the young man said politely: "Got to be getting on with this brute, he needs more of a stroll than yours does."

The wolfhound had stood all this time like a statue, his chin up and his eyes fixed on nothing. Rena said: "He's beautiful."

"Yes, nice feller."

Mr. Ordway smiled at her again, replaced his hat, and went off up the block. Rena unwound Aby from the garbage can, and followed at a distance.

As she and Aby climbed the front steps of the house, she hoped the Austens were down in the basement; if they were in the library Aby would rush in, and somebody—Jerome or Hildreth—would call to her. That was routine. They didn't like her, she was sure they thought Gray a fool to have married her, but they put up a show. Gray said it was her imagination. Even the servants ignored her as much as they could. And how they adored Gray, all of them! Rena had a good idea of the kind of thing they said in the kitchen: What a little nobody of a gold digger, to catch Mr. Gray, God love him.

The front door opened finally to her ring—Norah would have been in the basement getting the cocktail tray ready. The wrinkled Norah admitted her glumly; Aby dashed past for the library. Jerome's voice called to her in his patronizing way: "Hello there, Chick, come on back."

If she didn't, somebody would come upstairs after her. She left her coat and hat on the hall bench and went along the passage past the drawing-room on the right, past the basement stairs on the left, through the little dark square ante-room with its book-cases surmounted by busts of Roman worthies, into the big library.

It was always in a half-light, since one of its high windows was blocked by the house next door and one was inset with medallions of German stained glass. The open dining-room doors beyond sent in most of the light there was. Now in the dusk, with no lamps on and a low fire in the chimney-place, it was like a cave. She could hardly make out the three figures sitting around the hearth.

Hildreth's affected voice said: "Turn on a lamp, will you, pet? And join us. Almost time for cocktails."

CHAPTER TWO

Two Ways Out

NOBODY MOVED as Rena came and stood beside Gray's chair. He was lounging far back in it as usual, his braced leg out in front of him, cigarettes on the little table that would hold his cocktail and his canapé, a book in his hands. He looked very morose, and didn't lift his face to look up at her. His dark eyes were fixed on the fire.

Jerome sat in the middle chair, with Aby slavering at his feet: Aby knew that bits of toast and perhaps bacon would soon be coming his way. A hateful, conceited fellow Rena thought Jerome was; tall, dark, heavy and getting heavier, with thick jowls and a slightly overhanging upper lip. He had none of Gray's beauty or charm, but he had personality, no doubt of it. Hildreth was lighter than the others: rust-coloured hair and eyes, a sallow, freckled skin, shallow jaws, an ungainly figure;

her feet were clumsy, yet she always crossed her knees and had one foot out as if to be admired.

Jerome and Hildreth were talking about their trip home to settle up a deceased aunt's estate. Rena, looking down at her husband, wondered how in spite of his sullen moods she had ever fallen out of love with him. His narrow, pale face was so appealing, clear and regularly featured as a statue's; his eyes so beautifully set, his mouth so firm, his hair so smooth and fine. What was he reading? *Her* book—one of the few she owned. She kept it up in their sitting-room, and she didn't remember that he had ever noticed it.

She remembered very well how she had come to buy it. She thought of the day in the publisher's office where she worked, the day she had been sent into the editor-in-chief's room with a manuscript. The author was there, and several other people, and as she came towards the door she heard them all laughing. When she went in she saw that they were laughing at something the author had been saying; he was leaning up against the window ledge with his hands in his pockets, a colourless-looking man except for greenish eyes. If she could have expressed the impression he made on her, she would have said that he was entirely without self-consciousness or arrogance, but quite sure of himself; and that he was kind, but got a lot of amusement out of his fellow-creatures.

His manuscript was entitled: *Murderers Speak.*

"Thank you, Miss Seton," said the editor from behind his desk.

The author had thought it was "Seaton." He said: "My God, Miss Seaton, I hope you have no aunt?"

Somebody asked: "Now what? Why shouldn't she?" But she had answered him seriously: "It isn't spelt that way."

Then they had both begun to laugh, and he had said: "Miss Seton, I am your friend for life. Shall we send these people to night school?"

"I just happened—"

"I happen to read Walter de la Mare too. You tell me if an aunt or anybody else bothers you."

She had hurried out, smiling: and of course she had asked about him in the office, and they had told her a good deal. She had bought his book when it came out, and had enjoyed it very much. Gray never read such things, though; he never read all the interesting crime books up in their sitting-room. The bookshelves were crammed with them, trials and novels, old and new.

Hildreth was saying: "...and really, Gray, there's something to be said for a stiff knee. If it doesn't hurt, I mean."

"Think so?" Gray's eyes turned towards her, the whites showing.

"Alibis you out of anything."

"That's so," agreed Jerome. "*You* don't have to travel across a continent to collect seven hundred and fifty dollars and crate up a houseful of stuff that nobody wants. But you'll be paying part of the storage on it, my boy."

"Seven hundred and fifty all she had?" asked Gray without interest.

"I told you; she lived on the interest out of a trust fund, and the principal now goes to village improvements. I don't know how she ever saved the seven fifty, hanged if I do."

Hildreth remarked: "I can send for the stuff, Gray, if you ever get sick of me and want me to set up in a place of my own."

Gray said with a dryness unusual to him where his brother and sister were concerned: "I don't think Uncle's bequest would run to two establishments."

"Darling Gray, you know I was joking. And as a matter of fact some of that furniture isn't bad."

"Wouldn't fit in here," said Jerome, looking around him and smiling.

Gray said: "Throw it out as far as I'm concerned. This may be as bad as you and Hil say, but it suits me."

"Bad but fascinating," said Hildreth, "and very comfortable. Oh, the wonderful beds."

"Thank God Uncle liked you, old boy," said Jerome.

Nobody was paying any attention to Rena—did anybody ever? She went quietly out of the library, along the passage, and up the stairs.

It was a steep flight, and at the head of it, just before the turn for the upper hall, there was a railed landing. Access was gained to it by a gate from the hall, and it was lighted dimly by a ruby lamp in a lantern hanging by a chain. A big piece of imitation tapestry covered the whole wall space behind it, from ceiling to floor. It had been an "improvement," contrived at the turn of the century; it was in fact nothing but a large clothes closet with the rear wall taken away—the old door, opening into the sitting-room, could be seen behind the tapestry if anybody looked. It could be seen in the sitting-room, too, rather unfortunately extending up above the secretary that now stood against it.

Well, perhaps it did open out the view a little, thought Rena, climbing the stairs; and the legend was that stringed orchestras played on the railed landing in the old days of receptions, no doubt behind palms. It was of no use now, and it was like the rest of the house; something useless and rather ugly had been superimposed everywhere, or almost everywhere, on honest late-Victorian foundations.

Rena climbed to the upper hall, and turned in to the sitting-room. She put her coat and hat away in one of the two tall closets that flanked the built-in bookshelves, and went on back through the bedroom into the little dressing-room beyond it. She had taken off her dress in order to wash for dinner, when the dumb-waiter doors began to rattle—they seemed to catch every draught. They had kept her awake half the night before. She must find something to stuff up the big gap between them, caused no doubt by the warping of the old wood. They were half-doors, coming together with a flimsy bolt.

A couple of circulars might stuff up the crack, or thick letters, or folded newspaper. But when Rena went back through the blue-satin and walnut bedroom to the sitting-room, she found nothing of the kind anywhere. A thin paper-bound book, perhaps? She had seen one or two on those shelves. Here were two thin books, one paper-bound and one in morocco, tied together with faded old pink tape, crushed between *The New Newgate Calendar* and *The Trial of the Stauntons*.

She took them out; very dusty, quite old. The bound book was in half-morocco, red, faded; the paper book was faded too, coloured like dust itself. She came over to the light, laid the bound book on the table and began to clap the pages of the other, holding it well away from her slip.

Gray was coming up the stairs; she stopped, the book open in her hands, while he slowly climbed to the hall and slowly came into the sitting-room. He had her book in his hand, and he threw it aside on the table without looking at her.

"Don't think much of that," he said. Very well then, she wasn't going to inform him that she had met the author. He was always bored when she said anything about her work, anyway.

"I mean," he said, "who cares?"

"It seemed interesting to me."

"Morbid." He glanced then at the open book in her hand; and when he raised his eyes to hers, Rena had never seen such a look on anybody's face before. It was murderous. He snatched the thing out of her hand, looked down and saw the other, snatched that up too. He read the title, which was more than Rena had done. Putting one on top of the other, he raised his eyes again to meet hers.

"Doing a little research?" he asked. One hand fell away to his side, and she saw almost without believing her eyes that it clenched into a fist.

She stepped back. "Gray, what's the matter with you?"

His pale face was flushed now to his forehead. He looked down at the books again, and at her. She was completely terrified.

"Gray, are you going crazy? Why shouldn't I read them? And I wasn't reading them; I don't even know what they're about. I was dusting them."

He swallowed after a moment, and said in a husky voice: "Dusting them?"

"I was going to stuff up the crack in the dumbwaiter doors. You know how it rattles."

After another pause, in a different tone, he said: "No, I don't. I sleep at night."

It was at last too much for her; she said: "Gray, let me go. You don't want me. It isn't as if you really needed me. If you did, I'd stay. But I won't stay now."

If she had been frightened before, that was nothing to what she felt now. He took a step towards her, and the clenched hand at his side rose a little; then he suddenly turned, went out of the room, and slammed the door behind him. She heard the key turn in the lock.

Twice in the last few minutes she had been in actual fear of her life; this was as bad but different; she had never dreamed what it would feel like to be locked up anywhere. There was horror in it. To be helpless, to wait for that door to open again, to see that maniac's face of his—no. All in a moment she was galvanized into action by plain rage.

She looked all round the sitting-room, and her eyes fastened on the foot of disused doorway that showed above the secretary. She ran over and dragged at the side of the secretary—she could hardly move it, but it came out a foot at last. She stood peering in at the old door; the knob had been taken away, and when she put a finger into the big old keyhole and worked the door back and forth a little, or tried to, she was sure it was locked. Those old locks...three closets in the room... three keys?

No; only the closet nearest her had a key in it, a large heavy key. She got it out and tried it in the disused door, and the lock turned; what was more, the door swung open towards her; when the knob was taken out the spring that controlled the hasp must have been weakened. She could put her hand through and feel the smooth reverse of the machine-made tapestry.

She backed around the side of the secretary, whirled, and hurried lightly through to the dressing-room. She knew how little time she had; Gray had gone down to consult his brother and sister, those mysterious little books would be shown them. Then something would be done. But he had locked her in, and left her half-dressed and in a paralysis of fear; he might not think it necessary to hurry back.

She pulled her dress on, came back to the sitting-room and got her coat and hat out of the closet—she mustn't look too crazy on the street. Gloves and handbag she must have left down in the library. No time to look, no time for anything—she must be gone before Gray even thought she would try it.

That other girl, she thought, as she squeezed past the secretary, through the door, between the wall and the tapestry: had she been locked in? A thought followed by another, which seemed to come of itself—had she tried to get out by a window, and fallen, and had they hushed it up and called her death pneumonia? But no, Dr. Wolfram wouldn't—he had been old Mr. Austen's doctor, and he seemed a pleasant sort of man. She might go to him, but he was *their* doctor now, and it was too late. She knew where he lived, though.

Half-way down the stairs she heard voices in the library; Jerome's, raised in anger: "You obsessed fool, go up there and unlock that door and apologize." But that didn't mean they'd let her go. Well, if they tried to stop her now she could scream and make trouble—the servants would hear. They wouldn't like that.

She reached the front door, left it open behind her, and ran down to the street. Not a minute to lose now, and it seemed so far to the corner. She was half-running. Mr. Ordway and dog, coming along across the way from the direction of the park, saw her and stared. They crossed diagonally and caught up with her.

Ordway asked: "Trouble? Anything I can do?" and did not break his stride.

"I have to go. I have to go."

"Looks like it." He took in her set face from which all the bloom had gone, her fixed grey eyes, the bare hands holding her coat together. No worry here; plain funk, to him.

"You lamming out of there?" he asked as coolly as if such a thing might happen to anybody.

"Don't tell. Please don't tell."

"Tell? Certainly I won't tell. You need a cab."

They had reached the corner; a cab was pulling up in front of the apartment house, the doorman letting someone out of it. She gasped: "I haven't any money for it."

"That's all right, I have cab fare on me." He signalled the driver, who would have gone on home if Rena had been the one to signal him. He waited at the corner while Ordway followed the doorman up to the entrance, passed him Gawain's leash and a dollar bill: "Hold on to this boy for me, will you, George? Back in a minute."

The doorman knew him by sight, accepted the leash and put a finger up to his cap.

Ordway put Rena into the cab and got in himself. She said in a stifled voice: "Just make him drive away."

Ordway leaned forward: "Grab this light up and over to Park, and then we'll tell you." He sat back as the cab swung left. "I'm getting out any time," he explained in his equable way. "Just say the word. You'd better have a five in ones, wouldn't you think so?"

"I don't know—can't explain." She was barely able to talk.

"You don't have to. Seen you on the block lots of times," said Ordway. "Quiet type, minding your own business and being good to the old pup. I feel as if we were old friends. I feel as if you knew what you were about, and wouldn't run off just for the fun of it."

"Oh, it was too much. I had to go. I was too frightened."

"No good sticking around and doing nothing if you're frightened," said Ordway. "Better to run one way or the other. I've done it dozens of times."

The cab stopped at Park Avenue for the lights, and the driver looked around. Rena gave him an address.

CHAPTER THREE

Asking for It

GAMADGE'S HOUSE was one of a row of three-story-and-basement brick dwellings, on the south side of the street in the east sixties. His next-door neighbour on the left, an architect named Briggs, had converted his two top floors into four one-room-and-bath flats, and himself lived and had his offices below. He was like Gamadge, devoted to his home and averse to change, and therefore struggled against certain plans of Gamadge's which were laid before him in the late summer of 1949.

"If your family's growing," protested Briggs, who was a bachelor and fastidiously remote from such matters, "why don't you move to the suburbs?"

"Clara and I don't care for commuting."

"I always understood," said Briggs righteously, "that when people take on these responsibilities they expect to sacrifice their own comfort a little. The city is no place to bring up children."

"That's just hearsay."

Briggs couldn't deny that the Gamadges' young son seemed to be burgeoning, but he wouldn't say so.

"This proposition is strictly to your advantage," insisted Gamadge, leaning across Briggs' work-table to tap his pencil on amateurish blueprints of his own. "Why, you could punch the hole in the wall yourself; don't tell me you don't know where all your pipes and wires are. Clara and I could help you carry away the bricks."

"I am not a builder. When's this new one coming?" asked Briggs irritably.

"Around Christmas. We've just got to have that nursery, Briggs," said Gamadge earnestly. "We need our extra top-floor room for Henry's bondwoman, and the new one will have to have one of its own, at least until it's out of swaddling-clothes. Think how nice for you; permanent tenant, no bother any more with leases and arrears of rent."

"You think I let people in here who can't pay?"

"If anything happened to me Clara would stay on," continued Gamadge, "don't worry. And if the whole damn family was swept away, all you'd have to do would be to fill up the doorway again."

"Am I to have a nursery-maid and a pram cluttering up my halls and stairways? And my other tenants won't stand for a lot of squalling."

"How about those parrots of Miss Montague's that we had to telephone about every night for weeks, till she moved them out to the country?"

"She moved them," replied Briggs. "You can't board an infant out, or can you?"

"And my new nursery isn't going to be as vulnerable as you seem to think," said Gamadge. "Not on your life. The door of the flat that leads out into your hall will be permanently sealed, soundproofed if you like; I'll pay."

"Just the same," said Briggs with disapproval, "I don't think you have this new one on your mind much. Sticking it off on the top floor of another house. How about if we had a fire here?" and Mr. Briggs crossed his fingers.

"It won't be any farther off than any nursery is in a decent-sized establishment," said Gamadge, "which ours for our purposes is not. And stairs have no terrors for us, we have our elevator. And I've left you your choice," added Gamadge largely, "front flat or back one."

"Mighty nice of you. Well, I'll look at the place and see what's in those walls. You must be a millionaire, extra flat and two nursery-maids."

Gamadge rose, victorious. "Cheaper than moving," he said. "And this baby-nurse won't stay for ever; when she goes Clara will help out. She does now. Well, you've saved our lives, Briggs; but that fat woman you've got up there now—didn't you say she was leaving because she couldn't get up and down stairs any more? You might have a lot of trouble renting your top flats now that people don't like to use their legs any more."

"Don't fool yourself."

But Briggs didn't want to lose the Gamadges as neighbours; their house was kept up as well as his own, which was more than could be said for the one next to him in the row. It was *all* flats, and the steps and vestibule were a sight.

So it was that on the morning of Saturday, April the fifteenth, 1950, a smart nursemaid in cloak, cap and veil pushed a handsome little pram through a doorway in the wall of Briggs' third-floor back, pushed it through the Gamadges' third-floor back, wheeled it out into the Gamadges' upper hall, and squeezed it and herself into the little elevator. In the front hall the outfit encountered Gamadge, who was going out himself after seeing Clara and young Henry off to a private play group.

Gamadge smiled at the nurse and bent over the pram. He shook the occupant's hand.

"Don't know how it is," he said, " but I seem to take more of a personal interest in this one. I liked the first one all right too, but in a kind of academic way. Now this one—something about it. Looks like me, too, I think—going to be homely."

The nursemaid remarked modestly that you couldn't tell when they were so young. They often grew out of it. Then she looked startled, joined after a moment in Gamadge's shout of laughter, and pushed the pram through the front door which Theodore, Gamadge's old coloured servant, held open for her. Gamadge helped her down the short flight of steps, and watched her start off towards the corner with her veil blowing. The pram was only going round and round the block, for Clara thought the new one (and the nursemaid too) a little young to buck traffic yet.

Gamadge took a taxi down to the Public Library, went up to Catalogues, and spent a long time looking through files of cards. Long practice of his profession had not made him fonder of the research that was naturally part of it, and he was scowling when he brought half a dozen slips to the table nearest him. He made them out, elbow to elbow with other workers who ignored him as he did them, and at last carried them across to the reading room. He handed the slips in, and went to one of the long tables to take off his coat and hat, sit down, and wait for his number to come up. He sat down as far as possible from the one other man at the table, for Gamadge did not love the close proximity of his fellow-creatures for its own sake.

A youngish man turned from the counter with a book, hesitated, and looked in Gamadge's direction.

"He'll come here as sure as shooting," thought Gamadge, "sit beside me with all the other chairs to choose from, and end up by starting a chat." He had sometimes wondered whether privacy in itself seemed horrible to his countrymen, or whether it had taken on a kind of immorality in their eyes, and become a thing to assault and break up at sight.

Sure enough, the young man did advance towards Gamadge; but as he walked forward Gamadge saw that he dragged one leg as if the leg had a brace on it.

Gamadge sat looking at him; at the narrow, pale, expressionless face, the dark eyes, the dark brushed-back hair, the good clothes and the slender hands. The expressionless look was not a blank one—it might conceal physical pain or a permanent sorrow.

He came and sat down at the end of the table, with only the corner of it between himself and Gamadge, laid his book in front of him (it was an advanced treatise on physics of some sort, Gamadge thought after glancing at it), and said in a low voice: "I ought to apologize first of all. I happened to see your name on one of your slips in the other room."

"Oh?"

"I oughtn't to do this, I know. But I've read one of *your* books, and my brother had heard about you. Could I ask you something?"

"Certainly."

"Do you charge a lot for what you do?"

"Just the usual," said Gamadge. "I suppose you know what I do. I'm supposed to advise on disputed manuscripts and documents."

"Are you?" The young man looked astonished. "I thought you investigated things for people—quietly."

"I have, sometimes," said Gamadge. "If you want to know my fee for that kind of thing, it's nothing."

"Nothing?"

"I'm not a professional," said Gamadge. "I have no facilities and no licence. I only do that kind of thing, very rarely, for friends or their friends, or because I'm interested for reasons of my own."

The young man sat slumped back in his chair, looking straight in front of him; after a minute he said: "There was a whole chapter in your book about people who disappeared."

"Well, the point of the book was that murderers tell on themselves sometimes without realizing that they're doing it."

"I got that."

"Of course. Those disappearances were solved for that reason. There have been plenty of others, and I could only add my conjectures to other people's about *them*."

After another, longer pause, the young man said: "My wife disappeared yesterday."

"No, did she? That's tough," said Gamadge.

"I mean she simply went out of the house for no reason, and hasn't come back, and we—my brother and sister and I—don't know what to do."

"If you think she got into an accident, or was taken ill, there's exactly one thing to do—go to the Missing Persons Bureau."

"We couldn't—if she meant to go, I couldn't start the police on it," said the young man dully. "It wouldn't be fair to her."

"They'd be very discreet; they're your only bet," said Gamadge. "They have the organization."

"We wouldn't risk it." He turned his head slowly to look Gamadge in the eyes. "She's very young. I suppose it was pretty stupid for her, looking after a lame man. But we can't just do nothing, and I want to know where she is. It's a responsibility. I hoped you could suggest something. I only have an income, I can't touch capital, but I could—"

Gamadge said: "Quite out of the question, as I've explained."

"She had no money with her," said the young man. "No friends here that I know of, and very few anywhere else. She lived with her father till he died—outside of New Brunswick. My name's Austen, we're up in the lower sixties." His voice was urgent, but when Gamadge glanced along the table at the man at the other end of it, he lowered it again. "What's become of her? She was upstairs in the sitting-room, and then she wasn't in the house. She might have gone out of her mind."

"You certainly ought—"

"I won't risk publicity." Austen got out a card and laid it in front of Gamadge. "Couldn't you consider just coming up and talking the thing over with the three of us? We've got to do something. I came down here just to get out of the house."

Gamadge sat silent for a few moments. Then he said: "If it's thoroughly understood that I won't be able to find her for you, and can give you no advice except what I've given you already..."

"Just talk it over," said Austen, "just say what you'd do in my place if you couldn't go to the police, because those things leak out and I wouldn't trust them. The newspapers—Mr. Gamadge, she's only twenty. Perhaps it was my fault, I get in the dumps sometimes."

"Five o'clock," said Gamadge.

Austen got up. He said, his hands on the edge of the table, "I never could express myself. But—my brother and sister will—all I can say is, I was going crazy."

He picked up his book and limped away. Gamadge met the annoyed glance of the man at the other end of the table, murmured: "Sorry, not my fault," and at the other's nod rose in his turn to claim the books that had long been waiting for him.

He got home before noon, to find Clara once more setting forth. She said: "The group's letting out, and I'm off again, and I do wish Nanny would get back. This is killing me."

"Where's the baby's nurse?"

"Upstairs with him, naturally."

"Can you give me a few minutes in the library? I have something to talk over with you."

"I'll have to take a cab, then."

"They won't turn the child into the street. Just get hold of Miss Brown, will you?"

"We can't send her for Henry, she's been on her feet—"

The nursery-maid, however, was running lightly down the stairs from the top floor when Gamadge and Clara emerged from the elevator; Gamadge said: "A word with you, Miss Brown, which I think will interest you. I've just had the pleasure of a talk with your husband in the Public Library."

Clara exclaimed and seized hold of Rena's arm. Rena was gazing at her, unable to speak.

"It's all right," said Gamadge cheerfully. "He hasn't a notion."

"Hasn't a notion!" Clara was incredulous. "You mean it was a coincidence, or something? I don't believe it."

Rena said in a faltering voice: "He must have found out. And I was so sure Mr. Ordway…"

"He hasn't found out," said Gamadge, "and Ordway didn't tell. Come in and have some sherry."

Rena, on the chesterfield, drank sherry and listened to him; as he talked colour came back into her face, she leaned against the cushions relaxed, her hands lay quiet.

"He wanted to make out that it was a chance encounter," said Gamadge, "said he saw my name on one of my library slips. But he was lying, he didn't see it! So I thought it was ethical to meet him on his own ground—he was asking for it. I did assure him, though, that I wouldn't be able to find you. Have some more sherry! I know it's a shock, it was for me too."

"But I don't understand…"

"Perfectly simple. He'd read my book, as you told me; the brother did know something of what I've done, you say he gets around," said Gamadge smugly. "And they couldn't simply ignore your exit, that's true enough—Wolfram would wonder, the servants would wonder. And Austen does want to find you, you know."

She nodded.

"But quietly, no publicity. Oh, so quietly: so he took a shot at me. But the clumsy fool thought it would be more effective to do it like this, in his own indirect way. So he must have hung around outside the house, and seen me leave, and driven down to the Library after me."

"He has a car," said Rena. "He hardly ever drives it. Jerome does all the driving."

"Well, your husband drove this time, and I took so long to get through at the files that he had plenty of time to park and come in and catch me looking up titles in the catalogue room."

"But if he saw you leave—I left too!"

"Serena," said Gamadge, who liked her old-fashioned name, "you know why we put you into that uniform. It's the best disguise on earth, with that veil around your face and your hair under it."

"And thank Heaven you're in it," said Clara, "for with Nanny off to go to that family funeral, all I could think of was resting my feet."

Rena almost sobbed: "At least I can think I'm earning my food."

"If Nanny weren't getting back on Sunday night we'd make you go on slaving for us."

"I can't believe it yet. Coming here and telling you, and nobody saying I was crazy and ought to go back."

"Imagine your remembering me," said Gamadge. "I was flattered."

"Imagine your remembering me," said Rena, "as soon as I reminded you about Seaton's Aunt."

"Besides," Gamadge assured her, "it's a very interesting case. Right up my alley."

"I thought it was very strange there, but—"

"Oh, very interesting," repeated Gamadge. "Those books."

"Did you—"

"No, I didn't; I fumbled among murder cases all morning, and I never got within a mile of Mr. Austen and the pneumonia."

"Could it really be that?"

"That's all we have so far."

Clara said: "You'll get on with it, now you're so thick with him."

"Yes, I'm going up there to discuss it with the Austens at five o'clock this afternoon. I'm dying to go. He made himself very pathetic, Serena; sad story, and if you hadn't got to me first I might have shed tears over it."

"Perhaps I ought to be shedding tears over it," said Rena.

"Because you were fooled into marrying a man you didn't know? But it's puzzling," admitted Gamadge, with a frown. "Very puzzling, the whole thing."

"Oh, why didn't I really look at those two books! Clara, don't go."

"I have to," groaned Clara, getting up.

"*You* can't go," said Gamadge, addressing Rena with some sternness. "This new development requires a lot of new strategy, and we'd better get down to some questions and answers."

"The baby's asleep, but—"

"I'll send Rose up," said Clara. She hurried out, and Gamadge sat down at his desk and arranged papers.

"Now we'll go over it again," he said. "Things will unfold. Question one: why did he marry you at all?"

CHAPTER FOUR

A Marriage

THE BIG CHOW came into the room, acknowledged company with a waft of his tail, and retired to his favourite corner out of the way. Rena followed him with her eyes; when she met Gamadge's again her face was clouded with perplexity.

"You don't know either," said Gamadge. "You've asked the question of yourself a hundred times. Why marry you in the first place, if you weren't the kind of person he could go on being civil to for more than a few weeks? You know, Serena, it wasn't a rash, precipitate kind of marriage, cooked up on the spur of the moment over cocktails in a bar. You didn't go into it hurriedly and flightily. A month—that's not such a short time; Clara and I knew our own minds in less than a month, I can tell you."

"I meant it to be forever."

"Yes, and *you* didn't change. You wouldn't—anybody could tell you wouldn't, just by looking at you. And you stuck it out until he turned dangerous, or went out of his mind. He got just what he thought he was getting. Made no complaints afterwards, you tell me; didn't lament that he was disappointed in you."

"No."

"In fact hung on to you, wouldn't hear of separation, and now wants you back. You didn't change, I say; but what happened to him?"

"I thought his leg...the war..."

"Leg? Leg?" Gamadge shook his head. "Not enough in itself. Not nearly enough. Why, this Ordway, you tell me, is disfigured for life; and he seems to be taking it coolly enough. Of course you'll say that's not quite fair, it's a matter of temperament. That's just what I'm getting at. If he had the kind of character that reacted in that way, if after five years he still has some kind of war neurosis, then..." Gamadge broke off to light a cigarette. He sat back, smoked for a few moments and looked at her through the blue haze. Then he said: "If he's still mentally sick enough to be so badly affected after so long an interval, you ought to have been told about it. That was a deception, if you like! And he was aided and abetted in it by his brother and sister, who must have known."

"He never said anything."

"I don't believe there was anything of the kind to say. That affair yesterday of the books shows that his trouble is based on something besides nervous disorder. He's nervously disordered, all right, but that's the result of a definite fear or anxiety. He put up a front for seven weeks, and then when he had you tied up and safe, he relaxed. But marriage...and that repeated pattern in wives. It gets me," said Gamadge frankly. "It has me beat."

"Perhaps he would have changed sooner," said Rena, "if we hadn't been travelling around so much on the honeymoon. Afterwards I thought perhaps I would have noticed a change sooner, if—"

"Where did you go?" asked Gamadge.

"We all went in the car—down through the Southern states."

"All?" Gamadge stared.

A ghostly smile appeared on her lips. "The four of us, you know."

"You and Gray Austen and his brother and sister?" Gamadge's voice was full of something that half-choked it; when she nodded, he gulped as if unable for the moment to speak. Then he said: "I'll be hanged. Looks as if they didn't dare let him loose. Keepers. My God, are we wrong? Is he really as crazy as a...no. We're not wrong, and he isn't crazy; not yet."

"They explained," said Rena. "Jerome and Hildreth do the driving, you know, Gray doesn't care for it. They hadn't had a trip for a long time, and they told me it would save Gray so much money if they went with us instead of going off later by themselves. He laughed about it; he said it didn't matter to him, but as they didn't have much of any income themselves they were careful not to be more of an expense to him than they could help. *He* didn't care."

"He wasn't in love with you, Serena," said Gamadge. "He never loved you, not as I understand the word. You were fooled into that marriage, and I'm only sorry you ever felt the faintest remorse about breaking away. Now let's leave fruitless conjecture and get busy on those books."

"Fastened together with pink tape," said Rena.

"Yes, they were a pair of something; and as you know, a pair is always much more than twice as valuable as a thing alone. Chairs, candlesticks, vases and lovebirds. But you don't know why they were together, especially as one was in paper covers and the other bound."

"They were the same size and thickness."

"Octavos. And all you saw on the cover of the paper one was the word '*Case*'."

"It must have been a trial, Mr. Gamadge, because inside it was all questions and answers."

"Good. It was a trial, and we imagine that it was a murder trial, and Mr. Gray Austen hadn't known that it was among those other trials and cases on the shelves in the sitting-room. He didn't mind your reading the rest of them, you know; but when he caught the title of that one, he could have killed you for (as he thought) reading it. I wish to goodness you'd noticed what the other book said."

"All I saw was one word in big gilt letters: 'Summing-Up.'"

"You don't say." Gamadge was much interested. "We didn't get as far as that last night. That does make them a pair, doesn't it? A trial and then a summing-up by the judge."

"And the bound book was all in fine print, and double columns," said Rena helpfully.

Gamadge's eyes wandered. After a pause for thought he sighed. "They're hard to come by sometimes," he said, "those verbatim reports of trials; collectors' items, some of them are. But so many are not, and how can we ever… I wish we had an approximate date on them, Serena."

"I told you they were old."

"Yes, but damn it, how old?"

"Not really old," said Rena. "Old-fashioned."

"I know exactly what you mean. You wouldn't see that kind of paper cover or paper or type now, but it wasn't a curiosity. Not like this," said Gamadge, getting up to take a bound file from a shelf, and handing it to her open. She looked at the grey, rough-printed broadside, and shook her head. Gamadge laid it down and took an old catalogue from another file. "More like this?"

"Very *much* like it."

"Middle Victorian," said Gamadge, "and a good period for reports on trials. Lots of them were reprinted, you know, the best murders; *Notable English Trials*, and other collections, some right up to date."

"Some of those notable trials are in old Mr. Austen's collection. I read them. Fascinating," said Rena.

"Welcome to the Society. I have the best," said Gamadge, "and you're welcome to them. Read them to the baby. Of course you were going to stuff some of them into a crack; that's against you. But like your husband, you thought them insignificant and not worth reading."

"Won't yours help at all?"

"I'm afraid they hurt our case, instead of helping it," said Gamadge sadly. "I mean our case against Gray Austen for the murder of his first wife."

She looked at him silently, and did not protest.

"Scared you badly, didn't he?" Gamadge was biting his thumb. He released it, and mournfully shook his head. "They hurt our case because they're old."

"Because they're old?"

"The things that scared *him* were old things, perhaps a century old. They didn't know anything about killing people with germs seventy-five or a hundred years ago; and leaving people in draughts always was a tricky, unsatisfactory way of murdering them, and nowadays it's easier to cure pneumonia. You know, we'll absolutely have to get after that doctor."

"Wolfram? But he's a very nice man."

"We'll get after him, though, and the sooner the better." Gamadge reflected. "I'll put Dave Malcolm on him; Dave loves a problem, and he loves to make up stories; and he can work his way in anywhere."

"But won't Doctor Wolfram tell the Austens that somebody was asking questions about—"

"Leave it to Dave." Gamadge, frowning very much, looked down at the few notes he had been making. "Something gnaws at me," he said.

"Does it?" Rena, in sympathy, frowned too.

"On the outer edges of my consciousness. But I can't get at it, let it go. Let it go, and resign ourselves to the bleak truth; so far as we know at present, we shall have to read every trial of every case in old Mr. Austen's collection."

· "Why?"

"Because Gray Austen didn't mind your reading them. We can discover in that way what he didn't do—by process of elimination."

Rena looked aghast.

"At least some of the things he didn't do," said Gamadge gloomily. "And now for our last hurdle. You told me last night that you thought you convinced him you hadn't read those two little books; that you'd only been dusting them."

"I'm sure I convinced him of it."

"His manner changed, he calmed down. Then you said you wanted to leave him, and *that* seems to have been what stirred him up so much that he dashed out of the room and locked you in."

"I think I know why he behaved like that." Rena looked distressed. "I'm afraid I do."

"Let me in on it."

"Well, I referred to his leg."

Gamadge raised his eyebrows enquiringly.

"I said he didn't really need me, and I meant his leg wasn't painful and that he could get around with it. He knew I meant that, and it was just the last straw. He can't bear anybody to refer to it. I can understand. But he has it on his mind all the time, and he does expect people to remember it and make things easy for him."

"Exploits it," said Gamadge.

"Anyway, when I said I wanted to go, and said he didn't need me, he lost his head. He locked me in as much out of anger as anything."

"And his family realized that it was the wrong thing to do, and wanted him to go upstairs and apologize. They're in it with him, Serena, whatever it is. They'll have their story ready for me, you know, and it won't have any locked door in it."

"They'll say terrible things, I suppose."

"Oh, they're going to be very kind. *You're* the moody one; poor neurotic child picked up out of pity and married out of kindness; he was the one that had all the money and everything, and that's what you were after. You know, Serena"—Gamadge looked at her sideways—"I hope to goodness nobody will mention Ordway to them."

She flushed a little. "But I told you how careful Mr. Ordway was; that doorman never even saw me. It was wonderful, the way he managed it."

"He could compromise our case, you know. Bob Macloud, my lawyer, is going to take you on—or I hope so. We mustn't let *him* hear anything about Mr. Ordway; you're not supposed to have run off *with* anybody."

"But I don't even know Mr. Ordway!"

"As I said, it doesn't take long. I hope this isn't going to be another of your mistakes, Serena; you do jump to conclusions a little, you'll have to admit that."

"Well, I wish you'd seen him."

"I shall, don't worry. I shall."

"He didn't come in last night because he thought—he knew I hardly knew you at all, and he thought perhaps it would be less awkward for me to see you alone."

"Sensible of him."

"But he knew of you, Mr. Gamadge."

"That's nothing, I know of him. I know of old Mr. Austen, if it comes to that," said Gamadge. "The Native-born. They all know about one another, you'd be surprised. A big city, you think? Parochial!"

"He wouldn't have left me here if he hadn't been sure of *you*," said Rena reproachfully.

"What would he have suggested in that case?" asked Gamadge with mild curiosity. "I believe that he lives with his father—old shipping business—and I have an idea that his grandmother is still with them. And they live right across the street from the Austens. I hardly think—"

"He would have thought of something. He's like a rock, Mr. Gamadge. So steadying."

Gamadge said benevolently: "I'm sure he is; but we won't tell Macloud so. Now let me telephone to Dave Malcolm, and here's Theodore to lay the table for lunch."

CHAPTER FIVE

Nobody Calls on Miss Brown

LUNCH WAS OVER, the children had (as Gamadge expressed it) been put away, the animals were at people's feet; Gamadge, Clara and Mrs. Gray Austen had finished their coffee and were smoking. Theodore came to the library door with a card on a tray. He cast an enquiring look around the room.

"Who for, Theodore?" asked Clara, reclining on the chesterfield.

"The gentleman asked for a Mrs. Austen, ma'am. I tell him no such lady staying here, he say he want to see the lady came last night."

Gamadge, well back in an armchair with his eyes shut, said without opening them: "He's a little early; I expected him in say half an hour."

"I expected him this morning," murmured Clara. "But perhaps he has to work on Saturdays, junior partner and all. Did I go to one of his birthday parties once? If so, he poured café glacé down my neck."

"Funny, very funny," said Rena. "But I should call it only polite of him to call."

Gamadge opened his eyes. "Austen is Miss Brown's pen name, Theodore. Tell the gentleman..." With a start he sat upright and glanced around him. "Merciful Heavens, has he a dog with him?"

"I still has my senses, sir," protested Theodore.

"And Mr. Ordway's dog wouldn't hurt a fly," said Rena.

"Sun would, though," Clara informed her, "if the fly bothered him."

"Mr. Ordway's dog was wonderful about Aby, I told you so."

"Yes, but Sun wouldn't get behind ashcans."

"I wouldn't want to see that fight," said Gamadge.

"What interests me," offered Theodore, "is whether the gentleman is to come up, or whether the young lady will go down. My impression was that he wished to see the young lady and nobody else."

"He has no choice in the matter," said Gamadge. "Bring Mr. Ordway up here, and if she has any other callers—"

"Oh, don't," cried Rena.

"...any other callers," repeated Gamadge, "say she's not here under any name."

Theodore retired. Clara sat up and rearranged her hair. Rena watched the doorway.

Ordway came in, glanced about him, and was met in the middle of the room by Gamadge, who shook hands with him warmly.

"This is very nice of you," said Gamadge. "We were hoping you'd turn up to enquire after Mrs. Austen."

"Left her in rather a state, I'm afraid."

"She's all right now. Here she is, and let me introduce you to my wife."

Ordway shook hands with Clara, and then turned and looked at Rena in her cap and uniform.

"Mighty becoming," he said admiringly.

This reaction to the unusual delighted his host. "Serena was right," he declared, "you're unshakable."

"She say that?" Ordway smiled broadly at her.

"I never should have got anywhere without you. I should have sat down on the kerb till a policeman came and got me."

"Not at all, you did all right. I'm glad I happened to be around, though," said Ordway.

Clara begged him to sit down, which he did after looking to see that the chair would hold him. Gamadge offered cigarettes, offered a light, and then resumed his own seat.

"We owe you an explanation of the costume," he said. "Our regular nursemaid is away, and we thought her uniform and so on would be an excellent disguise for Mrs. Austen, in case any of the other Austens should happen to penetrate into this neighbourhood. As you realize, we're not so far away."

Ordway nodded, imperturbable.

"If you ask," continued Gamadge, "why she should be hiding from her husband and his relatives—"

"I don't."

"If you did, I should tell you that one of them seemed to be going out of his head, and frightened the life out of her."

"Knew she must have a good reason of her own," said Ordway.

"That's the proper attitude. But I must tell you, Mr. Ordway, that it's rather important for all and sundry to think she went off alone—as she meant to do. For instance: friendly as it was for you to come here, if you were known to be coming to see her..."

"I get it." Ordway rose to his feet. "Shouldn't have come. If you'll excuse me..."

Gamadge rose too. "No, no, you misunderstand. We're delighted to see you at any time; my wife thinks you may have poured ice cream in solution down her back many years ago."

Ordway may have been hard to shake, but Gamadge had now shaken him a little. He stared at Clara.

"You wouldn't remember," said Clara. "I was just one of those horrible little girls at your party. Please sit down again, Mr. Ordway, we only mean that when you come, it will be to see us. Not Rena."

"Oh. Yes," said Ordway. He resumed his chair, looking at Clara as if he expected to see trickles of something still decorating her collar. "Those parties. I don't seem to recall—"

"The name was Dawson; but never mind it."

Ordway looked at Rena. "I don't think anybody traced me here this time, but of course it wouldn't much matter if they did; because they didn't see us make our getaway last night."

"Somebody might have," said Clara.

"I don't think, myself," put in Gamadge, "that the Austens will ask around."

"I'll be careful."

"Just at present," Gamadge went on, "the less you know about the situation the better for all. So I won't—"

"That's all right. None of my business," said Ordway. "The thing is—I don't know whether I'll be out of line if I mention this—tell me to shut up if you like."

"Go right ahead."

Ordway glanced at Rena. "I was talking to my father last night about the family across the way," he said. "Naturally not about what happened, you understand."

"Quite natural," said Gamadge. "I'd have been a little interested myself, in your place."

"Well, my father knew old Mr. Austen and his father, both very nice people. And it seems that old Charles Austen's brother—can't remember his name—made a kind of bad start here or hereabouts, and cleared out west, and married somebody the family here didn't think much of. Old-fashioned," said Ordway, looking at Clara in a deprecating way. "So that might account for the fact that these people—that branch, I mean—seem so unusually lousy, excuse me for saying so. I don't mean the poor guy that got it in the leg. He seemed all right to me," and Ordway turned an anxious eye on Rena, "the little I've seen of him."

Rena said nothing.

"We're very much obliged to you for the information," said Gamadge briskly. "It accounts for a lot of things none of us, Mrs. Austen included, was able to understand."

Ordway now definitely rose. "Well, I just stopped in. I'm glad everything's—glad you had a good landing." He held Rena's hand and looked down at her. "Just let me know if I can—but I realize it's—don't want to make a nuisance of myself when the whole thing, as Mr. Gamadge says, is so…"

"I can't thank you," said Rena. "I don't even know how."

Gamadge took the visitor down to the front door. "We'll keep in touch," he said, "if you like."

"If I—you didn't see the getaway," said the young man. "That was something. What did they do, beat her up? She looked—"

"No, it was psychological."

"Worse than anything."

"And harder to put your finger on. I'd like to see that dog of yours, Mr. Ordway. Rena described him."

"Very nice feller."

"But I can't ask you to bring him here, unfortunately, because, as you may have noticed, we have animals of our own."

"Nice chow," said Ordway generously. "They say my feller could pull down a bear, but I wouldn't like to see him fight that chow."

Gamadge, recognizing this as the extreme of courtesy, bowed Ordway out of the house with respect. He went up to the library, put his head in, and addressed Rena solemnly: "It's all right, Serena, henceforth I shall defer to your judgment; your Mr. Ordway is an aristocrat."

Ordway walked home, climbed two flights of stairs to the third floor front, and went in. An old lady was sitting in the farther window, a book in her hands and the dog Gawain at her feet; from between her two sets of curtains she had a good view of half the block, and by leaning forward and craning she could rake the other half. She looked up.

"Hello, Gram." Ordway sat down opposite her and got out his pipe.

"Is that child all right, Norris?"

"Fine. Settled for the present." He began to laugh. "Seems their baby nurse is on holiday, and they've got her in the cap and veil and uniform."

"How clever."

"Wouldn't have recognized her myself at first, if I'd met her pushing the go-cart."

"It relieves me to know that she's getting out into the air; she's been looking very pale lately, and she's lost weight in the last months."

"They're a little worried about our being seen beating it away."

"You were not seen. That very disagreeable-looking maid of theirs didn't come to the front door and investigate until you were around the corner and out of my sight. I was relieved when I saw your cab turn, because by that time the others were all out in the vestibule."

"What I mean, Gram, they—Gamadge and his wife— seem to be cooking up some idea of a divorce for her."

"Naturally."

"And if I got into the picture they seem to think it might gum the works a little."

"It might. How about that doorman?"

"He didn't see her."

"They don't wish you to pursue the acquaintance, Norris?"

"I'm supposed to know *them*."

"Very simple. They must know something to the disadvantage of the lame husband. I thought he looked depressed when he came out to walk the little dog. It seems very sad. That brother—he's the living image of his father, poor old Charles Austen's elder brother, you know."

"What was that story, anyhow?" He added: "Dad mentioned something last night."

"Something about money; he was quietly pushed off the Stock Exchange."

"Thought they had plenty of dough."

"Not so much at that time; Charles Austen did very well for himself afterwards. Jerome Senior went west, and there was more trouble of some kind; and he married unfortunately. But this younger boy, they called him after Charles, you know—Charles Gray Austen; this younger boy did so well in the war, and he and Charles met before he went overseas, Charles Austen told me. Charles was much taken with him, and left him all his money for life."

Norris frowned. "It seems a mess."

"No girl of that kind would run off in that way without good reason," said old Mrs. Ordway.

"From what Gamadge said, I gather nobody ever laid a finger on her, anyhow."

"He wouldn't take her part for no reason, you know."

"Don't have to convince me." Norris Ordway smoked for a while, legs crossed, head against the padded back of his chair. His grandmother took up her book: *Le Temps Retrouvé.*

Presently Ordway said: "Those parties you used to give for me; birthday cake, magician with rabbit, magic-lantern slides."

"Yes?"

"Did they get out of hand at all? End up rough?"

"Naturally, dear; all the little boys."

"I can't remember much about them. Gamadge's wife—Dawson her name was…"

Old Mrs. Ordway raised her eyes from her book. "Beautiful child. I think there was a little accident—somebody upset some of the supper over her nice white dress."

"Oh. I was just wondering."

After another interval, speaking around the pipe, he said: "Austen had such bad luck with his first wife, too."

"Yes."

Their eyes met in a long, calm look. Then he observed: "Perhaps I ought to have carted *her* away."

Old Mrs. Ordway remarked that it might be just as well not to make a practice of it.

"You broke me of dumping the dessert down people's backs," said Ordway. "Or I suppose you did. I haven't done it lately."

CHAPTER SIX

Research

WHILE YOUNG ORDWAY'S past was thus being exposed to him, another young man, dark, perfectly dressed and limping a little, was shown into the office of Dr. Kurt Wolfram uptown. He had telephoned for an appointment, explaining that his own doctor was not available; which he wasn't, being at that moment on the golf course of his country club, using bad language about the weather.

The office nurse smiled sweetly upon the new patient, took his name, address and occupation all over again, said she hoped his knee wasn't painful at that moment, and feared it might be.

"It's better to-day," said Malcolm. "It was very bad last night."

"You don't sound as if it had bothered you this way before," said the nurse, with that little air of reminding one how lucky one is, for which her profession is famous.

"No, it hasn't," said Malcolm. "Can't understand it."

"You didn't try a little aspirin?"

"Is that a good thing to take for it?"

"It's considered so."

The nurse went away, and soon returned to pass Malcolm into a bright office. Dr. Wolfram rose behind his desk. He was stoutish and getting bald, and he had a thick blond moustache.

"Well, Mr. Malcolm; what can I do for you? You don't look as though you needed help from me or anybody. Knee bothering you?"

"Yes, this knee, Doctor," said Malcolm, indicating it. "The swelling's gone down, but it's still a little tender."

The doctor came around his desk to prod the knee in a way which would certainly have hurt if there had been anything the matter with it, so Malcolm winced.

"No blow? No injury?"

"Not a thing. The pain just came on yesterday afternoon, and hurt like mad for several hours. My wife finally gave me a pill; she needed some sleep too."

They both laughed. "These arthritic attacks are funny," said the doctor. "They come from nowhere and they go; but they go faster if you help them along with a few good big doses of aspirin every now and then. I'll write it down." He did so, saying meanwhile: "Liquid diet while you're taking the aspirin, and I recommend your going to a hospital and getting some thermotherapy if the attack returns."

"Well, I'm glad it's not serious," said Malcolm. "I had a vision of myself limping around like poor Gray Austen."

"Could end up like that," said the doctor, "I mean with a permanent affection of the knee joint, but not this time. Perhaps we'd better go into the question of diet, to ward off future trouble. Rheumatoid arthritis can be very troublesome." He went on writing, then glanced up to ask: "Know the Austens? What a shame that is for a young man; that *is* permanent."

"So I understand. I once knew his wife."

"Oh? Charming girl," said Wolfram, his face lighting up. "But the last time I was down there—Miss Austen's laryngitis, it was—I thought Mrs. Austen looked a little underweight. However, she never seems to be sick."

Malcolm said: "I mean Austen's first wife."

"Oh." Wolfram's face fell. After a moment he said: "Well, I'm glad the poor fellow consoled himself." He looked narrowly at Malcolm. "You know the poor little thing at all well?"

"Quite well, at one time." He added: "I was away when she died."

Wolfram shook his head and sighed heavily. "Couldn't shake it off, couldn't shake it off."

"Even at her age," said Malcolm. "I was a little surprised."

Wolfram said: "Well, of course, if you hadn't seen much of her of late years you *would* be surprised."

Malcolm had been heavily briefed, but he now found himself decidedly at sea. He judged it best to take a plunge: "I might have guessed, I suppose."

"No resistance," the doctor said.

"You see a good deal of that kind of thing."

"Not a stable temperament."

"No. No. That restaurant," muttered Malcolm.

"But Gray Austen assured me that she showed no sign of drinking when they married. Well, we all know these intervals. And the really sad thing was that poor Austen couldn't keep after her, being as he was crippled."

Malcolm wagged his head again.

"I felt very badly about that case," said Wolfram. "Truth is, she had no will to live."

"Almost like suicide."

"You could really call it that. Caught this severe cold from exposure, and got out of bed and out of the house twice to supply herself."

"Might almost have been more humane to keep it in the house for her."

"She'd have killed herself either way. Well," said the doctor, rising as Malcolm rose, "as I said, I'm glad he did better the second time. Quiet fellow, you wouldn't realize all he'd been through himself. Got that knee bailing out of his plane—I mean they shot him. Well, I hope you won't hear from *your* knee again, Mr. Malcolm; or from any other joint."

Malcolm paid his bill in the outer office and left. He took a cab to the Gamadge residence, where he found tea being served in the library. Little Henry and the animals were getting their share, and the baby was passed from lap to lap. Malcolm had it handed to him as he entered; he dandled it expertly while he reported:

"Wolfram's a nice man, I told him all about the wife's rheumatism and got all her remedies; she won't thank me for the news that nothing has changed in that ghastly little corner of medicine since her last attack. Wolfram is as honest as the day, and I had to exercise a good deal of histrionic ability to find out that the first Mrs. A. was a dipsomaniac. It seems to have started after marriage, and she seems to have brought her pneumonia on by her own unaided efforts, poor thing. Wolfram says she had no wish to live."

"Took to drink, did she?" Gamadge looked at Rena, who was listening horrified. "That was her solution. Well, it's one way out."

"I suppose he couldn't have managed it?" suggested Clara.

"Don't think so," said Malcolm. "Not the way Wolfram told it. She would get up and go out with a cold on her chest."

"The servants were on deck," said Gamadge, "and there'd be nurses."

Rena said after a moment: "I suppose until the pneumonia developed she'd be able to go out if she liked, sick or well."

"You mean those Austen servants wouldn't pay any attention to her?"

"Nobody would," said Rena in a low voice.

Malcolm, the baby over his shoulder, studied her in silence. Then he said: "Well, we can't fix responsibility, that's one sure thing."

Gamadge said with annoyance: "I'm stumped. Completely up a stump. She was our only bet, and Wolfram's ruined us."

"You did say those books made you think of something, Mr. Gamadge," said Rena.

"But the worst of it is, what they reminded me of wasn't anything that was *in* them," said Gamadge with a scowl.

They all looked at him blankly.

"I can't explain," he told them flatly. "It's like trying to remember a dream."

"But if what you can't remember isn't anything in the books," urged Clara, "then it must be what Rena said the books looked like."

"Not exactly."

Malcolm handed the baby back to Rena and stood gazing at nothing and rubbing the back of his head. "Then it must be because there were two books," he declared at last.

"That's the catch," said Gamadge. "What I can't remember is only about one of them."

"The trial, of course," said Clara. "The murder case."

"I'm not at all sure," answered Gamadge, his eyes roving. "In fact I'm almost sure not."

Clara cast herself down on the chesterfield; the baby, for the first time since Rena had entered the house, began to cry.

"I must have pinched him," she said, dazed.

Everybody was now in such a state of exasperation that even the younger Henry, getting the spirit of the meeting with the awful percipience of childhood, was peering up at his father in elderly disapproval.

The telephone rang and Gamadge went over to his writing-table to answer it. Malcolm collected himself.

"The big question now," he said briskly, "is when Miss Brown is coming to us. I understand that the children's authorized guardian is coming back to-morrow, and she mustn't find that her stand-in has been wearing her uniform—very much taken in at the seams, I imagine. There's lots of material for you to work on up in our place, Miss Brown; my wife can't wait.

She says to tell you followers are allowed, and you will have the usual perquisites: cocktails at the blue hour, and meals with the family. And Austen being such an admirer of Gamadge's, he might just drop in here and get past Theodore; whereas he never even heard of us."

"Such delightful notions you do have," said Clara.

"Gamadge will remember about those little books," continued Malcolm, "or, if he doesn't, he'll dig it out some other way. I know the old brain. He'll get Austen sent up the river, and by the time he gets out—life sentence because of his war wound—commuted for nice behaviour—you'll be married to some responsible character whose wives don't have to drink themselves to death or run away."

"You're getting a little ahead of us, Dave," suggested Clara. "Our Miss Brown isn't used to your realistic approach. You can see she doesn't care for it."

"All the same," said Malcolm, "she'll be the better for getting her mind on something else."

Gamadge returned, a half-sheet of notes in his hand. "That was Schenck, down in Washington. I got hold of him last night, and this morning he managed to look up Gray Austen's war record for us."

"Useful man," said Malcolm, "if you don't mind having the F.B.I. practically in the house with you."

"Captain Austen's career was blameless and better than blameless," said Gamadge. "Boiled down, it amounts to this: he was a fighter pilot, right through the war; his outfit ended up in the Pacific area, and he got that smashed knee towards the finish. First he was taken to hospital in the Philippines, and then brought by hospital ship to California; was in hospital there, and got his brace and everything, and emerged from there and from the army early in 1946. There was never a thing the matter with him, mentally or physically, so far as his command knew, and so far as the California people knew, except that smashed knee. No crack-ups, nothing. Seems to have been one of those ideal airmen. So," said Gamadge, looking up, "it would seem as though he'd developed the depression and so on—to be polite about it—after the war."

"Being lame might do it," said Malcolm, reflecting. "Byron is supposed to have suffered agonies over his lame foot."

"Deformed foot," Gamadge reminded him; "and he was born with it."

CHAPTER SEVEN

A Crime Book

AT FIVE O'CLOCK sharp Gamadge was in the vestibule of the Austen house, looking at a short, shrivelled maid in a plain apron; she had deep-sunk dark eyes, dyed black hair, and a mouth so puckered by wrinkles that it resembled the drawn-up opening of a reticule.

Gamadge handed her his card, which she received on her tray. He said: "They expect me, I believe."

"Yes, sir." Norah had a smile for any friend of the Austens', a smile which turned up the tight corners of the mouth and did not affect her eyes. She closed the door behind him while he took off his hat and coat.

"Any news of Mrs. Austen?" he asked.

"No, sir." Norah accepted the hat and coat from him.

"Too bad."

Norah was bursting with it: "Too bad! It is, and I say good riddance to her."

"You didn't care for her."

"It was not for me to care for her or not, but now I don't care for her, that's true," said Norah with a laugh. "Running away from her husband and him a cripple, God help him."

"He had such bad luck before, too."

"Worse than people know."

"*I* know," said Gamadge and shook his head.

"But you wouldn't know what it was like for the three of them, hunting her in bar-rooms. And meself, dragging her into the house when she'd be fallen in the vestibule."

"Dreadful thing, alcoholism."

"And her with everything. And this one—let her try to get a divorce and alimony from Mr. Gray! She'll have the three of us servants to contend with."

"And the three Austens, I suppose. Not a leg to stand on, has she?"

"The man's an angel. We're not used to the women running away from their husbands in this family," said Norah.

"The first one didn't."

"Where would she run to? Now this one, I dare say she had plenty of friends."

Norah turned and preceded him down the hall with pattering steps; but she stopped half-way and pointed upwards:

"Crazy, she was. Look how she pulled the picture off its hooks, and not a workman could we get over the weekend to put it up again."

The ruby light on the landing above them cast its livid glare on armoured figures and prancing horses; one corner of the tapestry hung down; Rena's story came to life for Gamadge as he glanced upwards.

At the library door Norah stood aside. Gamadge entered the big dim room, and Rena's story went on; but this time the three Austens and Aby were consuming a heavy tea. Jerome and Gray rose, Gray limped forward.

"Very kind of you, very kind."

"No news, I suppose, or you'd have let me know."

"Not a word. My sister, Mr. Gamadge. My brother Jerome."

Miss Austen smiled from her chair beside the tea table. Jerome shook hands, Aby advanced in two sections, as it were, his bulging eyes turned up to the visitor sideways. Gamadge stooped to put a hand on his head.

A chair was brought up beside Miss Austen. "And some hot crumpets, Norah, please," said that lady.

"Thank you very much, no; I've had tea," said Gamadge. "We gulp it down early—four o'clock."

Gray Austen wasn't looking at all well, Gamadge thought; paler even than he had been, and his handshake moist and yet cold. Very nervous. The brother seemed quite satisfied with himself and the world, and the sister in her rust-coloured dress and costume jewelry, her smart elaborate arrangement of hair, her fancy shoes, was the very picture of well-being and ease.

She said: "Let me tell you before we even begin to talk about Rena, Mr. Gamadge, that we've all read your wonderful book." There was some kind of eastern-seaboard accent superimposed on her natural way of speaking, with a result to discourage the experts. The same thing, Gamadge was amused to hear, had happened less drastically to Jerome.

Jerome, sitting down next to his sister, said: "We can give you something better than tea, you know. You don't have to follow our regime."

"It seems a pleasant one."

"We never touch a cocktail or anything else in the way of liquor before half-past six o'clock."

"I wish I could say the same for myself."

Miss Austen said merrily: "My brother means between lunch and half-past six."

"That's more human."

These two at least were not exactly in mourning for the loss of their sister-in-law, thought Gamadge, and not too greatly disturbed at the consequences if any. Gray Austen, however, sat gloomy and silent, feeding Aby with bits of crumpet, shifting the braced leg.

"You know," said Jerome, "we all feel very guilty about this business, as well as worried out of our wits. That good little thing!"

"We thought she was so perfectly happy," said Hildreth. "It shows how families are. Never notice these things coming on. She seemed very quiet, lately, but even that we got from Gray."

"Yes," said Gray. "She seemed quiet."

"Very young," put in Jerome, fatherly and benignly. "These moods—we forget as we grow older how urgent they are. No, Mr. Gamadge, we can't throw her to the police."

"I hope your brother explained," said Gamadge, "that I wouldn't dream of taking over? It's not a one-man job."

"It isn't as if she merely hadn't come home," said Hildreth. "In that case, of course, we should have called the hospitals—done everything. We simply want to be sure she's in safe hands somewhere, protected, and—most important of all—protected from the limelight."

Gray said in a husky voice: "I want to find where she is and talk to her. Find out what was wrong."

"Something must have been wrong, I suppose," said Gamadge, "I mean from her point of view."

"But the incredible thing is," said Jerome, offering cigarettes to his sister and then leaning across her to offer them to Gamadge, "that we'd just seen her. Just a few minutes before. She was quite all right then."

"Slipped out, though," said Hildreth. "We looked around and missed her, and Gray went up, and in a few minutes he came down and said she seemed very much disturbed and not herself, and we'd better go up and see what we could do. Mr. Gamadge, he was actually afraid to leave her at large!"

"At large?"

"I'd better admit what a fool I was," said Gray Austen moodily. "I locked her in."

"Oh." Gamadge, who had refused Jerome's offer of a cigarette, lighted one of his own.

"But I didn't mean her even to know it. I thought—I didn't suppose she'd even try the door. She wasn't dressed," said Gray Austen, turning his brooding eyes on Gamadge. "She hadn't her dress on. And in a couple of minutes Norah came in and said the front door was half open, and we went and—but you wouldn't believe what she'd done."

"Quite, quite mad at the moment," said Hildreth.

"Well…I shouldn't care to be locked up myself, dressed or not," said Gamadge.

"But she'd been acting so strangely! Gray," said his sister, "let's just take Mr. Gamadge up and *show* him."

"I locked the door," said Gray, his insistent gaze on Gamadge's, "because I was frightened myself." He got slowly to his feet. "And she did just what I was afraid she might do."

"Clears the voice," thought Gamadge, "to tell the truth."

The others had risen, and Gamadge rose. "You'll see what her state of mind must have been," said Jerome, "but only remember that she was worked up before. That's why Gray— we don't want him blaming himself."

"But I do." Gray was walking at his lame gait out of the library. "Coming on dusk, and she hadn't any money with her. Never had much—she could charge anything."

Hildreth said: "Wait, Gray darling," and Austen stopped. "I want to tell you something, Mr. Gamadge"—she fixed her eyes on his—"something about my brother Gray's character. You ought to understand him a little better before you go upstairs and see that door and that tapestry. Our uncle, Charles Gray Austen, left him everything; he died before Gray was out of hospital in California and left him this house and everything for life; Gray was named for him, you know.

"When I say everything, I mean everything except a sort of token to Jerome and me—a thousand dollars each."

She was very serious, but Jerome smiled. "Insurance," he said. "It's supposed to prevent disgruntled relatives from trying to break a will."

"But Gray," she went on, "insisted on our coming here and living with him; he even gives us an income. That doesn't leave him rich."

"Plenty for all," said Gray without turning.

"That's what my brother Gray says, plenty for all. Do you think, knowing what I tell you about him, that he'd be likely to be ungenerous in any way—any way—with his wife?"

"All this doesn't matter," said Gray. "What matters is that she said she wanted to leave me, and I locked her in."

"No reasons given for leaving you?" asked Gamadge, putting out his cigarette.

"None. She said"—he glanced down at his leg—"said I didn't need her. Well, I blew my top; come on up and see what she did."

He went ahead of them along the hall to the foot of the stairs and then stood aside for them to pass him. Jerome went first, Miss Austen next, Gamadge last; and in passing the lame man, Gamadge met his eyes.

"Unfathomable being," Gamadge thought, going up behind the Austen woman. For who could reconcile the large deeds of Captain Gray Austen with the meanness of his faults? If he were a wife-killer, or any other kind of killer, that would fit in better with his record than this cold hypocrisy. That was a wrench, Gamadge told himself, having to come out with the story of the locked door; but he couldn't avoid it—the servants would have got on to it when they got on to the other opened door and the curtain pulled off its nails. If they hadn't, Gamadge was sure he would never have heard of the locking-in.

This was a rehearsal; a story to meet Rena's story when and if she told it, something for an intelligent outsider to get well into his head, perhaps to act on. But there was more, probably much more to come.

Jerome stopped at the turn, looked over his shoulder at Gamadge, and indicated the tapestry at the back of the landing: "That funny little alcove, or whatever you could call it, is a fake," he said. "It used to be a clothes closet, believe me or not, and behind the fake tapestry is the door she got out by." He swung a leg over the rail, crossed the landing, and pulled the curtain aside. "See? It was locked, but she opened it with another key."

"And had to pull a great secretary away from in front of it," said Miss Austen. "I don't think I could have done it myself. The boys here think it was extraordinary of her to have thought of the other key—it belonged to one of the closets in the sitting-room; but I don't. Women are always locking things up and mislaying keys and looking for other keys that will fit; trunks, bags and boxes."

"Well, it was clever of her," said Jerome. He gained the hall through the little gate in the railing, and preceded the rest into the sitting-room. Hildreth Austen waved her hand at the old secretary, which had been pushed back almost to its original position and looked immovable.

"Just imagine," said Hildreth. Gray, leaning in the doorway of the room, seemed almost detached from the scene. Aby had laboured up the stairs after the crowd, and was panting and supporting himself against the braced leg.

Gamadge, his hands in his pockets, looked at the secretary, the top of the door that protruded above it, and around at the two tall closets. He said: "One sure thing—she wanted to go."

"Yes," said Hildreth. "Is it too awful of me—Gray won't hear of it—to suggest that she must have had someone to go *to*?"

Here it was. Gamadge swung to look at her. "Some man, you mean."

Gray said as if with small interest in the theory: "No. She had no one."

"But Gray," she besought him, "only think. She had a job at that publisher's."

"Not long."

"But why are you so obstinate? You didn't watch her letters. You don't know what she was doing every minute of the day. Mr. Gamadge will tell you that that's the first thing the police will ask—and believe, too!"

"Pretty little girl," said Jerome, taking some money out of his pocket and juggling it. "But I wouldn't have said—"

"Oh, you men!"

Gamadge had turned from the secretary; he was glancing about the room, and beyond into the luxury of the blue bedroom with its glimpses of looking glass vistas and flowered carpet. He said: "The police might think that the locking-in showed jealousy."

"And Gray hasn't a jealous drop of blood!" Miss Austen wailed it. "Now don't you see that we mustn't court publicity for either of them?"

"What's against the idea," said Gamadge, "is the abrupt manner of her going. She didn't even pack a little bag."

"She didn't even take her handbag," Miss Austen told him, "or her gloves, but if she suddenly decided—"

"It doesn't sound like that sort of decision, exactly." Gamadge's eyes met Gray Austen's again. "What did happen up here, exactly? After you came in."

Gray jerked his head forward. "She was reading something out of those bookshelves."

Gamadge walked over to them. "Was she?" He glanced along the shelves. "Nice collection."

"My tastes don't run that way, but she often took out a book. I went and looked; it was one of those ghastly rehashes of old murder cases, you know; people that chopped up their families and killed children and poisoned everybody with weed killer. I—don't see the sense of getting all that kind of thing second-hand; having seen a good deal of first-hand killing myself, you know. So I said something. Then she made me feel like a fool—she explained that she only had the thing out because she wanted to stuff up the crack between the dumbwaiter doors back there in our dressing-room; they'd been rattling. And I was going to apologize, and then she said she was going to leave me."

Hildreth drew a long sigh.

"And she seemed so wrought up," continued Gray in so low a voice that it was barely audible, "that I did the fatal thing. Locked that door." He had moved forward from it, and now turned his head to look at it with a kind of resentment. "If I hadn't, she'd probably be here now."

Jerome was blowing smoke-rings. He said: "Well, Mr. Gamadge, there you have it. If you can give Gray any private advice, well and good; you needn't commit yourself in front of witnesses." He smiled. "I don't agree with my sister. It was a tantrum, and she might be anywhere."

"In the river," said Gray coldly.

"Nonsense. Nonsense. Probably working it off—er—dish-washing. Independent working girl; proud little thing, I should say. If she'd gone off as you think, Hil, we'd have heard from her; if she's merely in a temper, we may never hear."

Gray said: "I have to know."

"Well, make Mr. Gamadge tell you, then." Jerome came up to Gamadge and shook hands. "Good luck."

"Thank you."

Jerome went briskly out of the room, and Hildreth came up to Gamadge in her turn. "I do hope we shall meet again in happier circumstances, Mr. Gamadge. And I hope you'll have something to drink before you go. Gray—you'll see to that, won't you?"

Gray nodded, and she withdrew smiling. Gamadge turned back to the bookshelves. Gray Austen joined him there.

"Very nice lot of stuff," said Gamadge. "That one, and that one—they're out of print. Booksellers have a standing order for some of these things; scouts always out for them. I'd give something for those two I pointed out, if you ever care to sell."

"Don't think I have a right to."

"That's so, life interest, your sister said. Well, at least you can read them. But you said you didn't care for criminology, I think. You know, you're wrong there, Mr. Austen."

"Am I?"

"I understand your personal reaction, but there's more to these murder cases and trials than mere slaughter and mayhem. Lots of human nature, and wonderful contemporary detail. Which collection was your wife reading when you came in here yesterday?"

"She wasn't reading it; I told you."

"Or said she wasn't," said Gamadge. "After all, you were scolding her; she might—"

"I believed her. Here it is," said Austen, pulling a thickish paper-bound book out of a shelf; thickish, that is, in comparison with Rena's description. It was limp and dog-eared.

Gamadge accepted it from him. "*Murder Cases Retold.* Very interesting; I remember this," said Gamadge, opening it at random. "Even in those days, in the middle nineteenth century, they sometimes had the sense to recognize that a doomed wretch was mad. Didn't execute him. These things are of interest to lawyers, you know."

"I don't think many people read them for the law in them."

"But this might be evidence for us, you know," said Gamadge, smiling at him and flipping pages.

"Evidence?" Gray Austen raised his eyebrows.

"We could determine by it whether or not your wife really was reading up old murder cases, or whether she was only intending to stuff up a crack."

Austen stood looking at him.

"It's rather thick for the purpose," suggested Gamadge, still smiling. "We might go back to wherever the dumbwaiter is, and see if it would fit in."

Austen, without moving his eyes from Gamadge's, said after a moment: "She might not have looked first."

"She'd have some idea."

"I don't care to check up on Rena." Austen took the book from Gamadge, and turned. "Here, Aby."

Aby squirmed towards him. He tossed the paper book to him, and Aby caught it in his mouth. He took it off into a corner, shook it to pieces at once, and began to chew the pages.

"Well!" Gamadge laughed. "What a gesture of chivalry! Dollars going down his maw."

"That isn't the kind of thing I want to know about Rena," said Gray.

"No. Well, let's see: what can I suggest that you don't know already, far better than I do? No police. No hospitals. No morgue. Where did you say she came from originally, Mr. Austen?"

"She was brought up in New Brunswick—near it. I have the name of the town somewhere."

"Enquire there."

"No friends left there, she said."

"But they know her."

"I might send my sister down," said Austen uncertainly. "A woman could do it better—without so much talk."

"Do nothing and you'll get nowhere. Find out who her friends were at that place where she worked before you married her."

"Cressons'."

"No, really? My publishers."

"The only girl she knew there at all well—the school friend that got her the job—is married and in Europe."

"You see how futile I am." Gamadge moved towards the door.

"Anyway, thanks. Jerome!" called Austen, limping into the hall. "Hey there!"

"Don't bother, I can get myself out."

"He might be playing a game of pool with Hildreth. Make you a drink."

"No, absolutely no." Gamadge was about to descend the stairs; Gray called upwards: "Hil? You there?"

"Yes, dear. Coming."

"Aby." He said morosely to Gamadge: "Rena took him out. He's missing it."

Miss Austen leaned over the banister of the third-floor landing. "Is Mr. Gamadge going? Just a minute, Mr. Gamadge, I'll go with you; let me get my hat on and find Aby's leash."

Gamadge went slowly down the stairs. Glancing at his watch, he saw that it was a minute or so after six o'clock.

CHAPTER EIGHT

Aby

GAMADGE AND GRAY exchanged a wave of the hand; Gamadge went on down the stairs, and Aby, with a dog's sixth sense concerning walks, humped after him like a measuring worm. Norah, alerted by some house bell, came up from the basement and brought him his hat and coat; but Miss Austen seemed to be taking her time. The three of them waited.

"The murderer speaks, does he?" thought Gamadge. "This one, if he is one, talks a lot too much. Can't understand him or any of it, except that last play with the book of crimes. He didn't much like me for that, Aby old boy. You were a godsend. What an idiot he is, overplaying his hand like that. But I have to remember that so far as he knows I'm hearing all *I* know from him."

Miss Austen came down at last, smartly got up for the street. She had changed her shoes, and she carried Aby's leash in a gloved hand. Aby plunged and fawned.

"Poor little boy," said Miss Austen, fastening the leash to his collar, "did oo miss oo Rena?"

Norah puckered up her mouth and opened the door.

Miss Austen was chatty. "You wouldn't believe it, he backs out of his collar. Such a responsibility. Oh dear," and she stopped at the bottom of the steps to look up at the sky, "I think it's snowing! Well, just a few flakes, never mind. Come on, Aby; which way do you go, Mr. Gamadge? Madison? All right, we go that way this time, Aby."

Everything was a dirty grey, from sky to street. They went along towards the corner.

"Perhaps you'd rather just try for a cab," suggested Miss Austen. "I walk in all weathers myself, the wild west, you know, don't laugh."

"Always glad of a walk."

"You go up? Then we needn't part company until the next corner north; with Aby, I'm only going around the block. He's so afraid of the traffic. But at this hour on Saturday there isn't so much, the theatres were out long ago and you don't see many people walking after the stores close. No, Aby."

He had made his détour to the ashcans in the service alley, but Miss Austen restrained him. "Isn't it all untidy?" she asked, pushing a cigarette end aside with her suède toe. And then, suddenly changing her tone and looking at Gamadge sharply: "What did you think of him?"

"Your brother?"

"My brother Gray."

"Well, he'd naturally be much disturbed."

"He's half-insane. That boy, Mr. Gamadge, is stoical—outwardly; it's his training. But—of course he thinks as I do. That she went off with someone. I don't mean that she meant to go at that very moment, she was dressing for it! But when he locked the door she was so angry—because she'd injured him, you know—that she just flew. Jerome is soft about her; man of the world, he makes allowances."

"It must be upsetting to be locked in."

"Think how upset he must have been to do it! So unlike him. If she hadn't meant to go, been all set to go, she'd have just banged or kicked the door."

A distinct mental image of Miss Austen kicking a door rose up in Gamadge's fancy as he looked at her. With her broad face and receding chin, her burnt-umber hair and eyes, her red-brown furs, she strongly reminded him of one of the lesser cats of jungle or mountain, translated into some Disney grotesque and kicking a door.

"But she didn't make a noise, oh no," continued Miss Austen, pausing with Aby at the corner. "So sly of her to find that other way out, and to do it all so fast."

The doorman of the apartment house had retired into the warm lobby; there was no one under the canopy as Gamadge, Miss Austen and Aby passed below it on their way up the avenue. Flakes of snow fell here and there, melting as they floated to rest. A few pedestrians hurried up or down the street, intent on getting elsewhere.

Next to the apartment house, and divided from it by a deep area that extended on into a narrow passage-way, was a yellowish, concrete building, an old relic mouldering and flaking away. There were stores, dark at present, on every floor but the top one, which had a look of shabby neglect from its crooked window blinds to the unlawful flower-pot on the sill. Some estate had it in a death-grip, no doubt, and wasn't wasting tied-up money on upkeep.

The area, railed off from the sidewalk, had steep concrete steps going down to the region of refuse cans below. Aby, fascinated by the look of the place, sidled up to the railing.

"Loves ashcans," commented Miss Austen, holding on to her fur toque with one hand.

The ashcans were congregated on either side of the steps, under which there seemed to be an empty space. Aby pushed his head between the railings and whined.

"No, Aby," said Miss Austen, jerking him. He backed out, ran around her, and made a try for the steps. Annoyed to find herself wound up by the leash, Miss Austen unwound herself by turning in her tracks like a dancer.

Aby barked in harsh short yaps.

"Rat, perhaps," suggested Gamadge.

"Urrh. Would there be?"

"Can't tell, in an old barracks like that one. Or perhaps he did see a rat there once, and has hopes always." Gamadge was rather touched that Aby's terrier instincts hadn't all been bred out of him.

"He simply won't come."

Gamadge went down a step or two and peered. He descended another step and another, and after a moment looked up at Miss Austen. She returned the look enquiringly.

"Somebody's in there. Perhaps I ought to see."

"Drunken man?"

Gamadge ran down to the area and leaned over rubbish bins. He pushed one aside and went into a dark, high, empty compartment roofed by the underside of stairs. The smallish, crumpled figure lay on its side, and there was something wrong with the back of its head. Gamadge hardly needed to put a finger on one wrist and into the hollow of the throat. Warm, no pulse at all. The body was dressed in slacks, sweater and belted raincoat.

He came back up the steps. "Fellow's dead."

"Oh dear."

"Just a kid, too. Had his head bashed in."

"How dreadful," said Miss Austen, looking pale.

"Hang on to Aby. Look here, Miss Austen, I have to turn in an alarm; would you like to beat it before I do?"

"Beat it?"

"I mean there'll be a lot of questions and waiting around and getting names. No reason for you to stay around in the cold."

"They're welcome to my name if they want it."

"You'll stay? You're a sport. Just sort of bar the way, will you? We don't want people going down there."

"Of course not." She stood at the head of the steps, Aby drawn up in front of her so tightly that he at last resigned himself and sat on her feet. Gamadge turned to look north and south.

A middle-aged man came along, carrying a brief case. Gamadge went up to him; they parleyed, and then the man, with a shocked glance towards the railings, retraced his steps to the corner. Gamadge returned and leaned against the rail beside Miss Austen.

"He'll send in the alarm."

"From the apartment house?"

"Yes. They'll be along in no time."

The man joined them, and in the circumstances Gamadge couldn't very well prevent him from taking a look himself; so by the time the police cars and ambulance came there was a little crowd, but nobody had got past Miss Austen and Aby, Gamadge and the fourth member of the original party.

The crowd thickened at the sound of sirens, and there was some pushing and shoving and a great deal of baseless information going from mouth to mouth and into the ears of the patrolmen and the detective from Homicide. Gamadge, staying where he was, had only a glimpse of the young man as they got him out from under the stairs and before they put him on the stretcher and covered him. Very young, perhaps twenty; with fair hair, a flattish undistinguished face, a brown sweater and slacks. He had had a smashing blow on the back of the head.

The young detective got around to Gamadge and Miss Austen at last. He glanced down at Aby with some disfavour— the dog had practically forced them into noticing the body, but couldn't answer a question except by drooling at the mouth and wagging his tail.

Miss Austen gave her name and address and was thanked and politely dismissed; she smiled and bowed to Gamadge, and went off up the street with Aby.

"Dogs must be walked, no matter what," said Gamadge, following the detective's eyes.

"That's so. Well, I guess I've got everything now, Mr. Gamadge. Thanks."

"Dead on arrival," said Gamadge, "but only just."

The detective looked at him coldly. "People lie around in doorways and on church steps, citizens think they're drunk. They mostly are."

"I know, it doesn't surprise me he wasn't seen before, or even that the murder wasn't seen. I meant—"

"Yes; thanks. That'll be all."

Gamadge thought it would be, unless some friend of his at the Precinct noticed his name on the report. He moved out into the open, to come face to face with young Mr. Ordway. Ordway hadn't his dog with him this time.

"Hello," said Gamadge.

"Hello. My grandmother said there seemed to be a gathering on the corner," said Ordway, "so I came out to see what was going on."

"Yes. Tell you what," said Gamadge, "it might be just as well if we crossed the street and wandered over to Park. Miss Austen is walking Aby, and she might take a notion to come around the block again."

"Oh." Without pausing for questions, Ordway walked with Gamadge to the corner and waited for the light. They crossed and proceeded east.

"What I mean is," continued Gamadge, "I've just been calling at their house by invitation, but they don't know I know Mrs. Gray Austen. Can't go into details yet."

Ordway jerked his head in acquiescence.

"Don't want them connecting me with you," said Gamadge. He added: "Just in case."

"They didn't see us together, I keep telling you," said Ordway, with a trifle of insistence in his tone. "My grandmother saw our getaway last evening—has her eyrie, you know. She's a good deal brighter than I am. Says the people didn't come out of there until we were well around the corner. She won't say anything. We haven't mentioned it to my father," he went on, with a sidelong glance at Gamadge. "He's a little old-fashioned."

Gamadge said laughing: "That's all right, only I wanted to impress something on you. The Austens are certainly going to make out that Rena ran away with a man. Now we know that's only technically—"

Ordway stopped and looked at him. "You mean I'd better not see her again."

Gamadge started him on with a touch on his elbow. "I just want you to get a look at the overall picture. Preliminaries aside, the usual stretch is now I believe only six weeks."

Ordway nodded gloomily.

"But of course," said Gamadge, "she could see a friend of the David Malcolms' if he dropped in, bearing well in mind the overall picture."

"Malcolms?" asked Ordway without apparent curiosity.

"She'll be there tomorrow afternoon at latest. They're in the telephone book."

"I appreciate this," said Ordway, his face a blank.

"The fact is," Gamadge went on, "I think very highly of Serena. She made one terrible mistake, and her friends don't want her to make another."

"Glad she has friends. It didn't look that way last night."

"She has nine now, including the baby," replied Gamadge. "Ten, including you. She'll have eleven in a short time, when my lawyer Macloud meets her."

"My grandmother wants to meet her."

Suddenly Ordway and Gamadge grinned in each other's faces. "That being that," said Ordway, "perhaps you could tell me what the excitement was back there."

"Glad to; I have a single-track mind," said Gamadge. "Boy was killed in the area."

Ordway turned a surprised look on him. Gamadge told the story, and Ordway thought it over in his deliberate way. At last he said: "Seems a public place."

"Well, I thought so; but the superintendent of that building never showed up—it's Saturday, and he might be off duty. Very few people on the street. Once get him down those steps—"

"That's so. It happened, anyhow."

They parted company at Park Avenue, and Gamadge took a cab uptown.

Macloud was expected for dinner; Gamadge was in his office conferring with Theodore on the state of the liquor department, when the telephone rang. He answered it.

Detective-lieutenant Nordhall's voice was lugubrious: "I hear you're using dogs now, Gamadge. Funny thing, I never had much success with them."

"You pick the wrong breeds."

"That's so, those Boston terriers were born snooping. Well, you behaved wonderful this time, I hear. Kept your alibi right with you, too—the lady."

"She was quite willing to stay."

"You deserve to hear all about the victim, if you're at all interested."

"I am, of course."

"Understand you came up pretty slick with the D.O.A. suggestion; Stevie Blitz hardly knew what to make of you."

"He gave me one of those looks; didn't need information that the young man was very recently dead."

"Poor Stevie, had he but known. Boy'd just been killed, had he?"

"Miss Austen and I were late by a few minutes, I should say."

"It's going to be hard to identify that little guy, unless somebody recognizes his picture and description when we get them out, and comes forward. No identifying marks on him, and nothing in his pockets, and his wrist watch had been taken. Signs of it on his wrist."

"Clothes?"

"You think labels stay put on that kind of old raincoat and that kind of slacks? Or on one of those twenty-five per cent wool sweaters? As for laundry marks, the kids now can take them and wash them in a public laundrette. He doesn't look local, the boy doesn't. Maybe a drifter, wasn't a bum."

"Can they tell at sight?"

"Pretty nearly. Mechanic's hands, and he was eating regular. Well, that's the way it goes," said Nordhall. "Any time, any place, and the motive a dollar's worth of change and a cheap watch. I suppose they'd have taken the clothes off him if there'd been time. As it was, plenty of room under those steps for a quick search. The killers were probably even younger than he was, to bother with him at all."

"Too bad, if he was such a respectable boy."

"Well, so long; give my regards to Miss What-is-it— Austen—when you see her."

"I was looking at some books they have."

"That so?" Nordhall rang off. Gamadge turned to call to Rena as she passed the office door on her way down to the kitchen.

"Whatever you do, Serena, keep that uniform on for dinner. Macloud's heart melts at the sight of a puir wee working lassie; he doesn't like members of the Lost Sex getting divorces."

Rena stopped and looked in. "Won't I still be a member?"

"Not in a bib and apron; not to Macloud."

"He sounds very frightening to me."

"He's only frightening to witnesses under cross-examination who are obviously lying to him. Did I tell you Mr. Ordway came in on the scene of the accident over on Madison?"

"No, did he?"

"Yes, and he says his grandmother wishes to make your acquaintance. How wrong I was yesterday! From what I can make out, the old lady would have welcomed you on Friday evening with open arms; and passed you off on Ordway Senior as her nurse-companion, brought in from the registry office by her ever-loving grandson. You know, it's very funny about the generations, alternating the way they do. Never fails."

Rena stood trying to follow him, her eyes squinting with the effort.

"Old lady and grandson adventurous," said Gamadge. "Ordway Senior has to have things kept from him."

"Yes… But you said accident," objected Rena. "I thought it was murder."

"Oh, on Madison. First lesson in the rules of evidence: rough kids wrestling around, as you often see them do, and one of them gets knocked down the concrete steps and smashes his head in. The others, cop-shy as usual, roll him out of sight and go home to their supper. Happens often."

"But do the police think—"

"What they think," Gamadge said, smiling at her, "is perhaps as far off the mark as the accident theory. There's Macloud. I hear the bell."

CHAPTER NINE

Short Cut

MACLOUD CAME UP to specifications. He was benign to Rena before and during dinner; and afterwards, sitting opposite her and drinking his coffee, which Clara poured while Gamadge distributed little glasses of brandy, his saturnine face still looked unusually bland.

"We might as well clear away the non-controversial business first," he said, getting his notebook out of his pocket.

"Mr. Macloud, I must tell you—" Rena choked on it a little. "I can't help what Mr. Gamadge says, you ought to know. I have no money at all."

"So I understand. You could get legal advice free, you know, Mrs. Austen," Macloud informed her with tolerance. "It's provided you. But as a friend of the Gamadges, I am delighted to advise you to the best of my ability."

"I keep telling her," said Gamadge, "that we're forming a company; lots of us already—I'm sure old Mrs. Ordway is well fixed, and Baby has a swollen bank account. And what does that remind me of?" He stopped with his brandy glass half-way to his lips and frowned at it.

"Your mind is evidently deteriorating," said Macloud. "First those mysterious books you talk about—and I'm not interested in them, Mrs. Austen; I know very little about the criminal law—and now a limited liability company; what do they remind him of? Let us have no more of these—er—'mere glimmerings and decays.'"

Gamadge swallowed the brandy.

"The trip west or south, and incidental expenses, is not prohibitively expensive nowadays, I believe," Macloud went on, "and an uncontested suit wouldn't be so either. But we will come back to that." He opened the notebook and found a page. "At present Gamadge is interested for some reason in old Charles Austen's will. I have an outline."

"Bob," said Clara, "I knew you would."

"Well, Clara, I know old Dabney the executor and I caught him at his home. He was quite willing to give me the gist of the will, because I or anybody could see it for ourselves on a week day; and he remembered all about it, because the estate is still in process of administration."

"That so?" Gamadge, leaning against his writing-table, was interested.

"As I am about to explain. You already know that Charles Austen took a fancy to his nephew Gray; had him to dine once at his club, followed his career as a flying man, and in 1945 made a new will leaving the boy his house and the income from his property, for life. On the boy's death this reverts to the original beneficiaries: public and charitable institutions in which the testator was interested, and excellent objects of interest they are."

Macloud lighted a cigarette and went on:

"Gray outlived him and got the house and the income; but a large part of the capital was tied up—about thirty thousand,

I think—for the benefit of an old family servant. He didn't die until early this year, and the Austen estate won't be finally wound up until early this summer. It's all plain sailing, you understand. And you will see, Mrs. Austen"—Macloud looked up at her again—"that if your husband meant to provide for you and for his relatives, his probable course would be to take out substantial insurance on his life. Dabney thinks the upkeep on that house, and personal expenses for three or four persons, would pretty certainly eat up the income, including what's coming in from that old trust. In fact, Dabney thinks they must have been a little pinched up to now."

"They lived rather quietly," said Rena.

"Just so. Well, to this action for divorce that you're contemplating."

Macloud's tone had become lugubrious. He put his fingers together and gazed at Rena as he might have gazed at a drooping plant or a sick kitten.

"We must remember," he said, "that your husband has five witnesses in the house, ready and willing to swear in any court of law that he was a model husband. He has Gamadge, brought in not of course as a witness to anything of that kind, because all Gamadge knows is what they tell him; but as a witness to the fact that Austen wanted his wife back, and wanted to find her in the most considerate possible way. In other words, that he had no resentment against her and sought no revenge, such as damaging publicity."

Gamadge was smiling.

"Now what have we, on the face of it?" enquired Macloud. "We have a good provider, who says he still loves his wife; he frankly admits the act which she construed as constraint of person, but he will swear—and so will his relations—that he only meant to leave the key turned for a few minutes, and that he only turned it because he was afraid she would give way to a fit of temper and run away on impulse; which, he will point out, is exactly what she did in fact do."

Rena swallowed, her eyes on him.

"As defendant in a contested suit," continued Macloud, putting his head back and looking at the ceiling, "he is decidedly an object of sympathy. He is a lame man, lamed in the course of hazardous service to his country; he is lame for life. He will contend that he needs the care and affection of his wife in these circumstances, and that she denies the very fact that he needs them."

"He doesn't," said Rena clearly.

"The balance of probability will be on his side. His story will be that you rushed away without giving any reason for going, and indeed secretly. Gamadge seems to think that there will be some suggestion that you were leaving to join a man. That," said Macloud, looking at her severely, "has no foundation whatever in fact, I presume?"

"It hasn't," said Rena, meeting his eyes. "Such a thing never entered my mind. I don't—I didn't know anyone, even."

"Good. Such things," observed Macloud, again to the ceiling, "can usually be dug up, if true. Well, I have given you as was proper the other side of the argument. Now for your side. In the circumstances, it is very much to your advantage that you are not demanding alimony. Some people, no doubt, will draw the conclusion from that fact that you have private means of support. I must advise Gamadge to be discreet in forming that limited liability company."

Gamadge seemed unperturbed.

"We have your unsupported word," continued Macloud, "that your husband had ceased to love you. He denies this flatly, and we must admit that the word 'love' does not always mean the same thing to different people. We have your word that on Friday afternoon your husband by the expression on his face, and by a not fully completed gesture, put you in terror of your life. He will deny it. That locked door, Mrs. Austen, the overt act, is your only visible means of support."

Rena sank back against the cushions. "I knew it," she said. "I always knew it."

"If he contests the suit—really, you know," said Macloud, breaking off to twist his head and look up at Gamadge, "I hardly wonder that you have been driven to the highly unorthodox course of trying to get Austen electrocuted. Short of killing the man off—"

Gamadge said: "You're wasting words on it. He won't contest."

"Won't contest? Mrs. Austen herself tells us frankly that he repeatedly refused to allow her to leave him. On Friday afternoon, that was the very thing that provoked the crisis, so far as we can judge what the crisis was."

"He won't contest," replied Gamadge. "He even hedged with me—spoke of her right to leave him if she wanted to. Can't you get it into your head, Bob, that he won't stand publicity?"

"So you say." Macloud leaned back again and smiled. "It's the bee in your bonnet—that he's committed a crime. But what the crime was, and why if Austen didn't want publicity he should by systematic neglect and subdued violence force her to leave him—"

"They're the kind of people," said Gamadge, coming over to sit beside Rena on the chesterfield, "who are so insensitive themselves that they can't recognize decent feeling when they see it. If Rena put up with things, they assumed that it was from self-interest. They never dreamed she'd give up the comforts of that house, and her nice clothes, and security, because she had nothing else from her husband. Miss Austen wouldn't quit a man for any such reason, I can tell you!"

Macloud thought this over, accepted it, and nodded.

"Rena stuck it out," said Gamadge, pointing at Macloud with his cigarette, "because she has a conscience and a sense of duty. She's a person who can make allowances for a man like Austen, and feel pity. But—as I make it out, and it's still very obscure to me—when Gray Austen married her he thought he'd bought a slave."

Rena said faintly: "I did feel a little—"

"This afternoon," Gamadge went on, "he went right on with the act. He showed me the morbid book you'd been reading, Serena. Only of course it was another one, and when I suggested trying it in the crack of that dumb-waiter door, he got rid of it in a hurry—threw it to the dog."

Clara, who had been sitting silent and receptive on Rena's other side, addressed Macloud quietly: "And wasn't *that* an odd thing to do, Bob?"

"It was," agreed Macloud.

"But you're not interested in those books, the real ones," said Gamadge, "although Austen looked ready to murder her when he thought she'd been reading them; although he'd got rid of them and had a substitute to show me because he's afraid she might mention them at some future time."

"Damn queer. But what can we do about it," asked Macloud, "since Mrs. Austen can't remember what they were, and you don't know and apparently never will?"

"I know one thing; Gray Austen doesn't like publicity, but his sister and probably his brother don't mind it at all. Rena says they got around; this afternoon she was quite willing to stay with me after we discovered that murder on Madison, and quite willing to go down on police records with me. They sent her on her way, of course, and they won't bother her again."

"Why should they? You of all people think they want to make work for themselves?"

"I'd really like to tell you why I think they should."

"Do."

Theodore came in to clear away the coffee things; Gamadge sat entirely relaxed, legs stretched out and feet crossed, one hand behind his head and the other hanging over the arm of the sofa with a cigarette between the fingers of it. He began to talk dreamily:

"It was a wonderful performance; the scenery, the timing, the lines. I didn't get the splendour of it at the time, because like the famous character who had never seen a play before, I thought it was real." He waited until Theodore was out of the room, and then added: "I didn't feel the truth creeping over me until Nordhall telephoned me about the murder after I got home."

Not looking at the three faces which were turned towards him, he talked on:

"We were all up in that sitting-room, as I told you; Jerome left us, then Miss Austen went. After a while, when I started to go, Gray Austen made it clear that he hadn't paid any attention to their farewell remarks to me—they both made it definite that I wasn't going to see them again that afternoon. Gray hadn't paid attention, so he tried to get hold of Jerome to see me out.

"That lets Gray Austen out; he wasn't behind the scenes of the show any more than I was. If he had been, he would never have called my attention to the fact that Jerome wasn't available. But Hildreth Austen was. At just after six o'clock she invited me to wait for her and Aby; I must have waited ten minutes. By that time Jerome had been off the stage for at least fifteen minutes or more.

"Miss Austen and Aby and I left. Aby likes to go first towards Fifth, as Rena said; but she steered him the other way. When we passed the service alley of the apartment house she professed herself disgusted with the litter on the street, although there was none except for a half-smoked cigarette. She squashed it with her toe and shoved it aside.

"We rounded the corner, and our progress was slow. Now here I must pause to do honour to Miss Hildreth Austen: to her mental agility and to her nerve. For I wasn't cast originally in the role I filled in the next half-hour; I couldn't have been, because they couldn't have known when I'd leave the conference with Gray Austen. Miss Austen just clapped the clown's costume on me at the last moment and dragged me on-stage with her.

"No chance of a hitch, you notice; if that signal hadn't been there for her—the cigarette end—she would have abandoned me at the corner and gone on around and around the block until Jerome did make a sign. As it was, she took me along with her through the big scene; and looking back on it, I couldn't tell you to save my life whether Aby would have hung on there at the railings or not. Anyway, we found the body among us—or rather I was pushed into finding it."

Now at last Macloud found his voice: "You're trying to say that Jerome Austen killed that boy?"

"I'm not trying; I'm saying so. Those two service alleys must meet at an angle back there. All he had to do was to go through from their street, wait for the boy, suggest the short cut, and do what the police say the thugs did. Afterwards he goes back, leaves the signal for his sister, waits around the corner of the alley, and when we pass by, goes home. Nobody was around on the Austen street, very few passed on Madison."

Gamadge stopped to put his cigarette out in an ashtray.

"Perhaps you'll explain," said Macloud in a restrained tone, "why."

"First I ought to explain that Jerome Austen wouldn't have done it if he thought there was any chance of the boy's being connected with that family in any way. As Nordhall says, he may never be identified at all; if he is, the identification won't involve the Austens."

Macloud said steadily: "Yours is the sort of imagination that gets a man into trouble."

"All right, all right," said Gamadge, "you're the one that's always accusing me of not telling you what's in my mind."

"If this is a sample...! You certainly love those people."

"I respect their sense of timing. Lovely. They expected the young fellow at the house at six, I suppose; Gray Austen didn't know he'd made the appointment, because Gray is a little nervous and jumpy at all times now, and what he doesn't know won't hurt him. Jerome took the telephone call or opened the letter. Ask Serena whether she's shocked at the notion that that brother and sister would murder to protect their meal-ticket from harm."

Clara exclaimed suddenly: "It's a brilliant idea. Henry! Of course. That boy was coming to blackmail Gray Austen about whatever he'd done before."

"That's so," said Macloud, laughing mirthlessly. "They're all murderers, the whole lot of them."

"There was something very wrong with them." Rena looked at him, very serious. "I always thought so. Waiting around, just waiting. I never could imagine what..."

"So we get back to the paper book," said Macloud cynically. "The paper book Gray Austen got the crime out of, only he'd never seen the paper book and didn't know it was there until Mrs. Austen happened not to be reading it."

"When he saw the paper book," Gamadge told him patiently, "he remembered that crime and realized that it was like his own crime, and being as I said nervous, thought his wife was refreshing her memory because she suspected him."

"He'd have killed Rena if she'd stayed. I know he would," said Clara.

Rena shook her head. "He believed me when I said I hadn't read the thing. How I wish I had!"

"Even if you had," said Macloud, "it might be something of a job to bring that particular crime home to Mr. Austen. He's lived thirty-odd years, and only been here in New York for four of them. Even the ingenious Mr. Malcolm can't seem to rake up evidence against him in the matter of his first wife's death."

"The other slave," murmured Gamadge. "She couldn't stand it either, and she couldn't face running away."

Macloud got up. "Keep me posted. I always like it when a divorce case gets settled in a nice way; but I hate libel cases, Gamadge, as you know, and I won't appear for you in this one."

"I promise not to breathe a word even to the police."

"Till you find those little books?"

"Till I find what was in those little books. The little books themselves are now ashes," said Gamadge, "unless they're being digested by Aby."

CHAPTER TEN

People Show an Interest

On SUNDAY MORNINGS the Gamadge household relaxed to such an extent that Gamadge, when he did get up, sat in his office with the doors wide to the hall; newspapers lay about on the floor, animals reclined on them. Theodore took his ease in the basement—the doorbell wouldn't ring.

This Sunday morning, however, saw Gamadge up and about at an unusually early hour. He had his breakfast alone, and then went forth into the greyness and chill of the streets. He walked over and up to the Precinct and asked for Nordhall. Nordhall, they told him, was at home. He was referred to Detective Blitz.

Detective Blitz remembered him very well, and greeted him with a certain reticence.

Gamadge said: "How are you? Nordhall called me up yesterday afternoon, when he heard I was one of the people who discovered that murder."

"That so?"

"We've been around together sometimes."

"Yeah, I understand so."

"I didn't mention it yesterday; no point in claiming acquaintance with officials in the department when it looks like a matter of routine."

Blitz said nothing.

"Seems so pretentious," continued Gamadge, resting his weight against a desk. "As if I wanted privileges and favours. I didn't need them. The Department handles these things all right, why bother them with unnecessary talk?"

"Sure. What can I do for you?"

"Well, I feel a kind of proprietary interest in the young man—"

"Nobody else seems to."

"Stranger, I suppose. You'll be keeping the body here until evening, as usual?"

"We keep them twenty-four hours and then send them down."

"I'd like another look at him."

"You'll be his first visitor."

Detective Blitz, not more taciturn now than was natural to him, preceded Gamadge down to the basement room where the dead youth lay on view. Gamadge stood looking down at a candid face with high cheekbones, light-blue eyes, a snub nose. There was no great intelligence visible in the face, and Gamadge thought that no matter how long the boy had lived there never would have been much.

"Scandinavian origin," said Gamadge.

"Guess so."

"Looks strong and healthy enough."

"Not as strong as the other guy."

"Still, a hammer or a wrench…"

Blitz smiled at him, the smile of superior knowledge. "This time the blunt instrument was the under edge of one of those concrete steps."

"No!"

"Feller got him backed in there talking, let's say, and then all of a sudden grabbed him by the head and slammed it back against the edge of the step nearest it. What a crack. Plenty of traces, but of course it's dark under there and *you* wouldn't have seen them."

"Never would have thought of looking. Did that one blow kill him?"

"Doc says it knocked him out, and then the feller finished the job on the pavement. Nothing else wrong with the kid at all," said Blitz, looking down at the subject with mature approbation. "Working kid, no disease, no scars or wounds, and he didn't dope or use much alcohol if any."

"He really ought to be traced."

"Well, those clothes of his—mass production. And he's too young to have been in the war. We don't think he'd have a record. Whatever there is, we'll have it pretty soon now, but... these boys get tired of where they are and what they're doing, sometimes; they cut loose and travel a long way. He wasn't down and out—he had that wrist watch, and his shoes are good enough. If he hadn't found a job around here yet..." Detective Blitz spread the fingers of one hand and turned the wrist.

"Funny for him to have been hunting a job in mid-town Manhattan."

"Seeing the sights; might have had quite some change in his pockets from his last job."

"Why on earth go down that area-way? No sights there."

"He might have been hunting the super, looking for a temporary handy-man job. The super wasn't there."

"Strikes me as a good time and place to pick for a murder, only you'd have to know about it," said Gamadge.

"Neighbourhood gangs know all about everything. Well, we probably will get something."

They turned away and went back up the stairs. "I'm very much obliged to you," said Gamadge. "The whole thing struck me as a little out of the ordinary, that's all."

"Glad to oblige. Lady all right?" asked Blitz at the station entrance. "Must have been a shock to anybody like that."

"Haven't heard. I don't know the people very well."

Gamadge walked home, to find the Malcolms there and Rena packing. "They got me things at the drugstore," she told Gamadge, "and this is somebody's nice little bag."

"Mine," said Gamadge, looking at it anxiously. "You're welcome to it."

"If I can only get some work soon!"

"Not yet; don't for mercy's sake show yourself."

"They're going to take me out in their car at night, and walk me somewhere. If I could only just *say* what I feel—about you all."

Elena Malcolm, appraising Mrs. Gray Austen's hat, dress and fur coat, muttered to Clara: "He didn't spare expense. Too bad she couldn't stick him."

"She stuck him for a year, and you should have seen her on Friday, when she came." Clara shut her eyes at the memory. "A wreck. Almost too frightened to talk."

"How about this Ordway character we're supposed to be such friends with?"

"Well, he helped her get away; but he didn't know her at the time, and now he isn't supposed to know her at all."

Elena Malcolm screwed up her eyes and looked at Clara with amusement.

"But he's so awfully nice," said Clara, "that we think he'll keep her cheered up a little."

"Certainly the stuff to give the troops. You and Henry will kill me sometime."

Rena, dressed and ready to go, turned and looked up at Gamadge. He took her hands.

"Keep the chin up, Miss Brown. You'll be hearing from me, I hope. I'm going to a psychiatrist about those books."

"If I only could do something for you. I'd do anything."

"May take you up on that."

Malcolm reported that the street was clear, and rushed the visitor across the sidewalk to his car. The three drove off waving. Clara went upstairs, and Gamadge retired to the office and dragged newspapers out from under the dog and the cat. He was immersed in them when the doorbell rang, and didn't emerge to close the office against the world. So when Theodore reported that a lady wished to speak to him he could only get up and face the lady as she came in.

Theodore said afterwards that he didn't know Miss Austen was going to push by him like that, or he would have got hold of the little dog. As it was, the unpardonable happened. Aby, untaught in the ways of polite animal society, tore his leash out of Miss Austen's hand and made for the cat Junior; Junior, hideously startled but instructed by his instincts, bounded from a chair to the top of the celestial globe and balanced there, spitting, like a trained tiger. The chow looked up, rose, and walked curiously up to Aby to get some kind of line on him. Aby stopped barking, began to whimper pitifully, and crept into the well of Gamadge's knee-hole desk.

"All right, Sun," said Gamadge, picking Junior up into his arms. "The little doggie didn't know."

Sun retired to his corner and lay down. Junior clawed himself free and bounded through the laboratory and away. Gamadge looked at his scratched hand and then with a forced unnatural smile at Miss Austen.

She said, much flustered: "Oh, I'm so sorry. You mean they actually—that dog and that cat actually—"

"As you see. Good morning, Miss Austen. Do take your things off and sit down." He closed the office doors, and came back to find her luxuriously spread out in one of the deep chairs.

"I was just walking naughty Aby," she said. "I dropped by to hear whether you'd heard anything more about the dreadful thing that happened yesterday."

"Of course you'd be interested." Gamadge sat in the other chair and offered cigarettes. He lighted one for her, observing with admiration that the fur coat had been changed to-day for a short fur jacket of the newest cut, that she had a little feathered hat to match, and that there were real topaz earrings on her ears. And on her fingers, as he noticed when she took off her glove.

"I can only stay a moment. How nice that detective was, wasn't he?"

"Yes, they're getting a very promising lot in the Force these days."

"Have they found out who the poor boy was?"

"Not yet. They say over at the Precinct that sometimes they never do manage to identify the victim."

"How very sad. I thought they had such wonderful ways now of tracing clothes."

Gamadge couldn't look at her. He fixed his eyes on the copper-plate over the mantel, and wondered why Sun the chow didn't forget his training and fly at her. Just checking up to make sure, was she? Jerome wouldn't have had much time or space to really roll the boy. He nearly told her not to worry.

"They may yet, of course. It's a question of the right people reading the description or seeing his picture, or reporting to the police. If nobody cares, nothing happens."

"Well, at least two people have taken an interest. I saw the papers this morning, and they said very little about it. Didn't mention our names," said Miss Austen, smirking at him. "Just the name of the gentleman who sent in the alarm for us."

"Well, they took his name at the Precinct when he called in; had it on their files for the newspapers. We got away from the scene before the press arrived."

"Not a very interesting tragedy, I'm afraid. If he'd been a pretty girl, or somebody in the news, I suppose he'd have been all over the front page for days. Columns and columns, and more than you'd expect sometimes." Miss Austen philosophized, moving her hand to make her rings flash in the firelight: "Such odd people they sometimes choose to make a fuss over. Something catches the public interest, I suppose. What do they call it? An 'angle'?"

Gamadge did not reply; he sat looking up at the picture like a man of stone; she waited for a few moments in surprise, then rose.

"Well, I must be going. I really must."

Gamadge sprang to his feet. He got Aby out from under the desk, shook hands, and said he supposed they hadn't heard from Mrs. Austen.

"We should have let you know. If I'm right, that theory of mine, you remember, we ought to hear on Monday morning."

"She'll certainly have to get in touch, or her lawyer will."

"Gray will die of it, I'm convinced of that. We're trying to persuade him to take a trip, I'm such a believer in travel as a cure-all. But..." She shook her head.

"Going to try New Brunswick?" Gamadge went out to the front door with her.

"I don't know."

Gamadge shut the door after her, and then stood looking at it. Clara came down the stairs.

"My goodness, Henry, that was a narrow escape!" He turned slowly. She said: "Did it scare you out of your wits? You look so—what's the matter?"

"I thought that little beast had got Junior, and then Junior sank his claws into me when I rescued him."

"Let's see. Oh, it's not bad. Have some iodine." She was puzzled. "What's upset you so?"

"I'm not upset. Miss Austen put ideas into my head, and they're still whirling. But getting into a focus, getting into a focus." He was grinning at her. "I've been a blasted fool."

"Henry! You remember about those books. I know you do."

"I remember about those books."

"What were they? What were they?" She had him by the front of the coat.

"Just what Serena said they were. I got it by an association of ideas, and it's for the record. Let me go talk to Nordhall."

"But I must know!"

"Come with me and listen in." But when he rang up, Mrs. Nordhall was not optimistic:

"Mr. Gamadge, I don't dare. He's having his Sunday sleep."

"Etta, it's so urgent."

"Well, O.K., but he'll be foaming."

"Yell my name at him and then go off and hide somewhere."

Nordhall came to the telephone, and he was put out indeed: "It had better be urgent," he fumed. "You loll around all day, and I work all night."

"I went over to the Precinct and looked at that boy."

"What of it? Can't you discover a homicide now without losing your head over it?"

"I just thought I might be able to put you on to the killer, Nordhall, if you'll help out a little."

"And I thought for once you told all." Nordhall interrupted himself with a deep yawn; Gamadge was indignant.

"Just because this lad wasn't a member of café society, you don't take an interest."

"All right, make it interesting."

"Sit down, it's a long story."

Gamadge put his elbows on the desk; Clara leaned over his shoulder. He talked for some time. After a while Nordhall began to make remarks, short and pointed.

"Clara's listening," said Gamadge, and went on.

When he had finished, and Nordhall had commented, the latter spoke doubtfully: "I'll put it up to them. But if we waited—"

"Nordhall, we mustn't wait."

"This will take some time; you can't get such good co-operation Sundays."

"Working through police you can, you know that. And we needn't wait, don't you understand?"

"Blitz could manage what you wanted this afternoon, that's easy; and you say you can take the risk of—I don't know."

"Nordhall, it's plain there's no danger there."

"People blow up sometimes."

"Not these people. Don't pretend you don't see the beauty of it, and what we can't risk is a getaway."

"Well, I'll start right in on it, set things going; and as far as I'm concerned I'm in. You'd better meet me downtown right after lunch—say in an hour."

Gamadge looked hastily at Clara and looked away. "All right, I'll be there."

"One thing—how did you get on to it all of a sudden?"

"That's a tale for a long winter evening."

He put down the receiver and let out a long breath. Clara said: "I'll go and tell them to get you something to eat now."

"Thank you, my angel." He dialled again. "Malcolm?"

"Right here."

"I want to speak to Miss Brown, please."

"She's busy."

"For Heaven's sake, he's not to overdo it."

"He seems solid. Wait a minute."

Rena came to the telephone. Gamadge said: "Rena, I'm taking you up on that promise you made me this morning, and I admit that I seem to be in rather a hurry about it. You said you'd do anything I asked you."

"So I will."

"I want you to go back to that house to-night."

There was a silence.

"Is it too much?" Gamadge's voice was gentle. "I know it's a lot. But you won't be there long, and they won't lay a finger on you; and I'll be outside with a policeman in a car, and so will Malcolm, I'm sure."

Her own voice was faint: "Why must I go?"

"Just to pack a bag; you said you needed things."

"They'll try to keep me."

"Not on your life. You have friends waiting outside for you, you have a job to go back to, and if they make a row about it they'll get in the papers. I know it's tough, Rena, but I can't get the evidence I want in any other way."

"What evidence?"

Gamadge told her.

CHAPTER ELEVEN

Incredible

AT HALF-PAST EIGHT on Sunday evening Rena Austen rang the bell of the Austen house and stepped forward into the vestibule. Her gloveless hands were clasped tightly together at her waistline; her eyes were fixed on the ground-glass pattern in front of them as if to imprint every leaf and every flower on her mind for all time.

Norah opened the door and stood there transfixed, as Rena seemed to be. The two looked at each other silently until Norah found words:

"So you're back. I might better shut the door in your face."

"I came for some of my things, Norah."

"I'll bet you did."

"Let me in, please."

"Not till I have me orders."

Jerome Austen spoke from the dark entrance to the drawing-room on the right: "Why Norah, I'm amazed at you. Let Mrs. Austen in."

Norah stepped back. Rena moved slowly forward into the hall, and turned her head to look at the man who was smiling at her. He seemed bigger and stouter than she remembered him, a figure of menace. Norah closed the door, and the slam was terrifying to Rena's ears.

"I just came back for a few things," said Rena mechanically.

Jerome began to laugh. "No, I don't believe it," he got out between guffaws. "It's incredible."

"And so it is, sir," said Norah.

"Never mind, Norah, just forget it," said Jerome. "Go on, now."

Norah walked back along the hall and was swallowed up in the dark of the kitchen stairs.

"I'll go up," said Rena.

Jerome stood grinning at her and wagging his head. "Incredible," he repeated. "A nice well-brought-up girl like you. Don't you know it isn't done? When you desert, it's for good; or else you come back to apologize and stay—if your husband will have you. You don't drop in for your toothbrush, you know."

"It isn't your business, Jerome."

"That's very true." He lifted his head, and Rena's eyes followed to where Gray stood leaning on the railing at the head of the stairs. The red glow from the lamp above him made him unrecognizable.

"You heard this, Gray?" asked Jerome in a rallying voice.

"I heard it."

"Want me to get them up from the basement to help with her trunks and bags? She has quite a lot of loot up there, you know. Nice ring on her finger, too; some callous females would have pawned it before they'd have the gall to drop in and ask for more."

Rena said, looking up at Gray, "I couldn't get things over the weekend. Not even gloves. I thought you wouldn't care."

Jerome was roaring with laughter again.

"All right, Jerry," said Gray. "That's all of that. Come on up, Rena. Glad of the chance for a talk."

"I can't stay."

"That's what you think."

She began to climb the stairs. As she neared the top, her husband came through the little gate to meet her in the hall; with the red light no longer on him he still seemed strange. She realized that he had been drinking, but that wasn't it; when, facing him in the sitting-room, she suddenly understood what the difference was, her legs weakened under her. He put out his hand to grasp her wrist, and if he had not grasped it she might have fallen.

"Where did you go? Where have you been?"

She could answer quite calmly: "I went to some people that knew somebody at Cressons'."

"Sounds intimate. What kind of people," he asked, his voice rising, "take strangers in off the street?"

"Their name's Malcolm; you can find them in the telephone book and call up, if you like."

"Just visiting, are you?"

"No. I work there."

"What at?"

"I'm a domestic servant."

He dropped her wrist to stand back and get a good look at her. "A what?"

"I take care of the children, for one thing."

"By God, a resident sitter!" He laughed, but added: "Not that I believe you."

She said: "Gray, I only want a few things, and my smallest bag."

"Oh yes, the forty-dollar one."

"I'll take them in paper, or a box, if you like. Just some things out of the dressing-room; my toilet things."

"You'll go on using them *here*."

"They're waiting for me in a car; Mr. Malcolm drove me down. Gray, you don't understand—these people need me."

"Jerome was right, you're incredible. He can go out and tell your friends that you have a previous engagement."

"I had to tell them that I'd left you, Gray; if I don't come pretty soon they'll make a terrible row."

"Call the man on the beat?" He laughed again. "He'll soon tell them how far he can get into a man's house without a warrant. Let them wait all night if they like."

"But it will make such a scandal, Gray."

He stood staring at her.

"And Mr. Malcolm never cares what they print; he's on a paper. He'd just think it was a joke, getting me out of here."

For a moment she thought he would kill her; but then his breathing came more regularly, he dropped his raised hand to his side, and limped away to the couch under the windows. He lay down and closed his eyes.

"When I picked you up off that park bench," he said wearily, "I didn't think it was a trial marriage."

"Neither did I."

"A year! Well, don't try for alimony."

"I don't want it."

She went back through the bedroom, past the great walnut-and-gilt bed on which the first wife had died, into the dressing-room. The little bag was in one of the high cupboards, and she got it out. She was flinging things into it from the medicine chest, wrapping bottles and jars in cleansing tissue, when Hildreth came to the door. Rena paid no attention to her, but went on packing.

"I thought I'd supervise this," said Hildreth.

Aby came in, went over to Rena and stood looking up at her. Had this indulgent deputy come back to stay? It hardly seemed so, she was putting things into a bag—no dog likes that kind of thing. Rena said in a toneless voice: "Hello, Aby." He wagged his stumpy tail.

Hildreth said: "I don't think those friends of yours—your employers—quite realize the situation. Jerome is explaining it to them. You may find yourself stranded."

Rena stood up straight. She said: "Please let me go by, Hildreth. I want a change of underthings and a nightgown."

"I remember the ones you came with," said Hildreth, following her into the bedroom. "Not much like these."

Rena got a few things out of a drawer and crushed them into the bag. She snapped it shut, and then for the first time looked fully at Hildreth Austen. The woman's face was purple.

"There's something behind this," she said. "I always thought so."

Rena went out into the sitting-room; Gray was still lying on the couch, his head turned away; Rena noticed for the first time that an open Gladstone bag was on a corner table, half-packed. She barely glanced at it, and was crossing to the door when he spoke:

"Rena."

"Yes, Gray," she said without turning.

"I can't make this out, any of it. Could you explain before you go?"

His tone was that of a man merely asking for information. She said without turning: "You frightened me."

"One display of temper? Haven't I an excuse to lose my temper sometimes?"

"It's all right, I suppose, if people care for each other." She went out and down the stairs, opened the front door, descended the steps. Malcolm stood at the door of his convertible; Jerome, hatless, lounged beside him with his hands in his trouser pockets, a patrolman had wandered up and stood swinging his club.

"That the lady?" asked the patrolman, looking at Rena with some amusement.

"That's our cook." Malcolm came across the sidewalk and took the bag from her. "Tell the officer you're leaving voluntarily, Mrs. Austen."

Jerome said with a smile: "We concede it. Well, it looks as though you'd get your wages regularly, Rena. Nice car."

"I could make a note of this," offered the patrolman, with a humorous look at Jerome.

"Quite unnecessary." Jerome stepped away, Malcolm helped Rena into the car beside his wife, and got in himself.

"Good night, all," said Jerome, grinning.

"Good night," said Malcolm.

The door slammed shut; the patrolman walked on towards Madison, Jerome went back up the steps and into the house, Malcolm drove to Fifth Avenue. The patrolman reached the corner and put out his hand; a police car started up and came around into the street; it followed Malcolm's convertible into Fifth and down, stopping behind it on the park side, where lights were dim. Nordhall and Gamadge got out, leaving a sergeant at the wheel. They went up to the convertible, and Malcolm handed out Rena's little bag. Nordhall took it from him tenderly.

"All O.K.?" asked Gamadge, putting his head in. Mrs. Malcolm laughed shortly; Rena was sitting back with her eyes shut, but she opened them at Gamadge's voice.

"Yes. He's packing."

"Packing! Not so good."

"It's all right, he had a fitted bag. And I saw that he'd taken what he wanted out of the medicine chest."

"Fine, then. Did they scare you half to death?"

"Yes; but—I know now, Mr. Gamadge. I *know*."

"Bars down a little?" he smiled.

"Yes. And they're all on wires. I could feel it as soon as I got into the house."

"Tell you one thing," said Nordhall, "I wouldn't take the risks this Gamadge takes."

Mrs. Malcolm, looking grim, said: "I wouldn't either. We'd better get home with the wreckage; I don't mind saying I'm a little wrecked myself."

"Let's go," said Malcolm.

Rena leaned forward, and she and Gamadge exchanged a smile; hers pale but loyal, his affectionate. The car started. Gamadge and Nordhall returned to theirs and got in. Nordhall placed the little bag carefully on the shelf under the window.

"Better hustle back there, from what she said," Nordhall told the driver. They started down for the next intersection.

"We'd have to go back anyway," said Gamadge. "It's on the cards. He's been working up to it."

"He stayed put so far, though. I don't know what set him off now. Nothing she did, anyway—if she's right."

"Do you think he hasn't been worrying right along about those books?" asked Gamadge. "He can't *know* she wasn't reading them. Now there's been the murder—"

"You keep insisting he wasn't in on that."

"But he certainly knows about it now, and that makes him an accessory."

"Perhaps he isn't starting tonight at all," grumbled Nordhall. "We might hang around till morning."

"You know better."

The car turned east. Nordhall lighted a cigarette. "I don't like getting out of the groove this way," he said. "If we could only wait—"

"What for? The rest of it is just check-up and anticlimax," said Gamadge with irritation.

"So you say. My God, Gamadge, I wish I could be as sure as you are."

"Didn't I convince the boys downtown?"

"Yes, but they didn't know he was going to skip."

"Can we let him do that?"

"I suppose this trip of his fixes it."

They were silent until the car turned uptown to stop across from the south corner of the Austen street. They had a good view of the house, and they were none too soon; a cab came round into the block from Madison, stopped, and Jerome got out. The front door of the house opened. Norah appeared, carrying a Gladstone bag, Jerome went up the steps and took it from her, and she retired to give place to Gray Austen.

He was wearing a soft hat and a topcoat; as he came slowly down the steps the cab driver got out and came around his car; he and Jerome helped Austen in, his bag was put in after him,

Jerome shut the door and the driver climbed back behind the wheel. Jerome went up the steps and into the house as the cab went off towards Fifth Avenue. The police car turned into the block and followed.

"Did he get a plane reservation?" mused Nordhall. "What's he catching Sunday night?" And then, after an interval of silence: "Goody, it's Grand Central."

The driver, who was anxiously watching his prey, had swerved east.

CHAPTER TWELVE

Leg Iron

THE CAB MADE THE TURN into the station entrance, and a porter got Austen's bag out. Then he helped Austen out, and the cab driver was paid and drove off. The police car waited until Austen and the redcap had gone in through the doors; then Nordhall spoke to a starter, and the three followed into the terminus.

They watched at the top of the stairs while the porter put the Gladstone bag down and Austen went over to a ticket window.

"Picking up his reservation," said Nordhall. "Where's he going to on a Sunday night?"

"There's the Owl to Boston," said Gamadge. "Twelve-thirty, Sunday nights only."

"That's quite a wait for him."

"I only suggest it because I know the train, and Boston is a good jumping-off point to almost anywhere. And he might think it would be very misleading to start so early and then take so late a train."

"How about his spending a night in a hotel, and taking off with the crowds to-morrow morning?"

"Perfectly all right, he has his disguise."

"In reverse," said Nordhall, laughing. "Well, it's a break for us, his taking the trip; his folks won't be expecting him to-night."

Austen came back from the New York, New Haven and Hartford window and spoke to the porter, who walked off in the direction of a checking office.

"You're right, it's going to be quite a wait for him," said Nordhall.

"He'll make for a dressing-room."

"Better go after him now, perhaps."

The porter came back, was tipped, and went away. Gray Austen was in no hurry to leave the concourse; he stood almost alone near the information desk, lighting a cigarette; traffic was thinning for the night.

"Just stay here for now, Ryder," said Nordhall to the sergeant. "We don't want to make it a gathering." He and Gamadge walked down the broad stairs and across the concourse. Austen had turned, and was limping towards the ramp. They caught up with him.

Nordhall touched him on the arm. He looked around, saw Gamadge, and stepped back a little; his face was expressionless.

Nordhall said: "We have no warrant yet for your arrest, Mr. Austen, but I thought you wouldn't mind having a little talk with us just the same. All the stuff will be coming through to-morrow, and one of our men took your picture this afternoon while you were walking the dog, and we have your fingerprints."

He stood staring.

"So as you can imagine," said Nordhall cheerfully, "it's only a question of time. So why shouldn't you get a statement in first, before the other two start talking? We have reason to think that you may not have had a hand in that murder. Looking at it one way—it's the way Mr. Gamadge here looks at it—in spite of being the whole show, you could be considered something of a cat's paw."

The blank gaze moved to Gamadge's face, lingered there as it were incuriously, came back to Nordhall's. Shock, thought Nordhall, he can't work it out yet and can't even try. But was it shock exactly or entirely? That blankness was so absolute; there was a kind of innocence in it.

Nordhall was conscious of a something like a withering at the edges of his confidence. "Not an atom of proof in our hands," he thought, "not even evidence. Perhaps not even fingerprints. What ever made me go at it this way?"

But he knew, he knew. Long tough training kept his eyes from Gamadge's, kept him from turning his head by a millimetre in Gamadge's direction. But his wordless communication, or perhaps his silence itself, got an answer.

Gamadge said pleasantly: "He might like to take that brace off first, Nordhall; he must be sick of it."

The young man shifted a foot. He said bitterly: "I haven't had a walk for four years, except now and then in the middle of the night." And he added: "I had the thing off to-night when Rena showed up. I thought I walked the same, but she looked for a minute as if she noticed something. Did she get my fingerprints for you? I don't know a thing about a murder."

"Now, now," said Nordhall, functioning again with zest. "Of course you know about it. Young fellow came here to see you, and Jerome headed him off. We'll certainly tie the boy in sooner or later; he must have been somebody Captain Austen knew out there. What's *your* name, by the way?"

"Tom Bayles."

"Mr. Bayles. Only a kid of sixteen, this boy must have been when he knew Captain Austen, but you may remember him. Let's go down to the lower level, what do you say, where we can sit and talk? You don't have to do any talking, remember, I'll do it."

Bayles said, looking down at his leg, "I wouldn't have let you get a hand on me if it wasn't for this."

"That's silly."

"I was just going to take it off."

"Mr. Gamadge thought it would be a nice kind of disguise for you—just not walking with a limp, sprinting around as good as anybody. You thought if anybody got after you the word would be out for a lame man?" Nordhall shook his head.

Bayles looked at Gamadge, looked away. "How does he get into it?" he asked shortly.

Gamadge said: "Serena got to me first."

Bayles showed anger now for the first time; he looked at Gamadge with the expression, Gamadge thought, which Rena must have seen and which had driven her out of the Austen house. "Why, the little—she did read those books then. Of all the cheating, lying—"

"That's funny," said Nordhall good-humouredly, "coming from you. Let's go down."

He raised a hand to signal the sergeant, and the three walked over to the stairs and descended into great reaches of emptiness. Nordhall steered Bayles over to a bench beside a closed gateway; they sat down, Gamadge on Nordhall's other side. The sergeant joined them and leaned against the wall with his arms folded.

"As I said," Nordhall began, "we'll have all our dope on Captain Austen to-morrow; it's army stuff, and they can afford air travel; the C.O. will fly in—only being Captain Austen's C.O., he won't know you or you him. Different outfits, I suppose."

Resting head and shoulders against the marble, his chin sunk down and his eyes half-closed, Bayles looked three-quarters asleep. Reaction seemed to have stupefied him. He felt in the pocket nearest Nordhall, said with a faint smile: "I have no gun on me," and got out a cigarette case with a monogram in gold.

"Not on this side of you, anyway," agreed Nordhall, returning the smile. "I noticed as we came downstairs. The sergeant is keeping an eye out, there on your right."

"Oh. It's in my bag—my service gun. Don't know why I brought it along; it isn't much of an argument in my case. What were you saying?"

"You and Captain Austen were in different outfits, I thought."

Bayles lighted a cigarette and smoked as if in a dream. "Yes, different outfits. We were in the same hospital, though, out there on the coast. There wasn't much the matter with me, I'd picked up a bug and I had combat fatigue," He looked at Nordhall sternly.

Nordhall shook his head. "Bad thing."

"So Austen and I got to be pretty good friends in there, and when I got my discharge I hung around and waited for him. I had no special plans. I have just a sister and an aunt in Illinois, don't see much of them. Never did, I mean, since I grew up. So..." his voice drifted off.

"So you waited around for Austen," said Nordhall.

"Till he could navigate with the brace on. By the time he got used to it we were both out of the army. He got a car, and asked me to ride out to Oregon with him, have a little fun on the way. We had the fun, and by the time we got to a wormy little town near Portland we hadn't much pay left. You must understand," said Bayles, "Austen was tough. Very tough. Nice feller, but tough. He'd put up a good show for his uncle, though, the one he was named after, and he'd been left this big income and the house; but the estate wasn't paying off yet.

"We'd been bumming around a good deal, as I said, in all kinds of towns and auto camps and motels—you can imagine. He began to complain of this earache. No more doctors and hospitals for him, though. He was bound to go on through to meet his brother and sister and buy a big car, and drive to New York. But he came down flat on his back in the wormy little burg, in a motel, and I had to send for Jerome. And the first thing Jerome noticed when he got to us was that the management hadn't sorted us out; thought I was Gray and Gray was me. It tells you something about Jerome's brains when I say that he didn't correct the people; because by what I'd said, he was pretty sure before he ever reached us that what Gray had picked up was meningitis."

The young man broke off, to explain: "We didn't look alike, you know; but we were both dark and about the same height and build, only he was heavier. What made it really so easy for us was that they'd sent a representative down from San Francisco—the executors had—to see him in the hospital and do all the identifying and put all the preliminaries through; and on our trip he was drunk so often that he showed me how to forge his signature to cheques and so on. We had a lot of fun out of my forgeries. I don't think he'd have been any more shocked over this game the Austens and I put up than they were. It's a tough family.

"Well, when he died in that dump, it wasn't only the manager that wanted him buried quick and no publicity; the town authorities were delighted to get rid of him and us—I'd been exposed, don't forget. They cut all the corners they dared to, and pushed us out. Gray was buried there under my name, and my folks were notified and didn't show up; why take the trip?

"By that time of course Jerome and I—and the sister, too—had it all fixed. They wanted that income as badly as I did. It was all plain sailing for me, naturally, with the Austens right with me and backing me. We never had a minute's trouble anywhere along the line."

His voice faded. When he spoke again it was with bitterness: "I don't say I would have turned the proposition down, even if I'd realized which end of the stick I was getting. *They* were all right—they could go anywhere and make friends, they were the real thing. But I—it never entered my head at first how it would be. I couldn't take a chance, not even drive a car, because no surgeon could ever take a look at my leg. I wouldn't dare go around at all, because I might meet somebody that had known me in the air force or anywhere else. And not only that—his picture couldn't get in the papers, any more than mine could; no publicity for Gray Austen, and no freedom to do a thing." He looked down at his leg: "This thing had got me.

"Well, it wouldn't be long, we thought. When we got the estate settled, I'd simply travel—go off somewhere for good, cash my remittances; *they'd* be safe, all right! The three of us had a deadlock on one another.

"And then we found out we were held up by that trust fund, and as we had nothing but the income from the estate split three ways, we didn't want delay. So I stayed on. Until June..." He put his elbows on his knees, dropped his cigarette to the floor and stepped on it.

Gamadge said after a moment: "You married, Mr. Bayles."

Bayles looked up at him sideways without raising his head. "No risk there," he said. "Not that I could find out, and I was pretty careful."

Nordhall asked sharply: "Why do it at all, much less twice?"

He answered quite simply: "I had to have *something*."

"Something." Nordhall turned to look at Gamadge. "No wonder one of them took to alcohol, and the other one had to run away."

Bayles sat up to stare. "Don't know what you mean."

"We mean," said Gamadge, "that your approach was deceptive; but then you couldn't very well explain that there wasn't any sentiment connected with the business."

Something in his tone brought the young man to his feet. "That's none of *your* business," he said loudly.

Gamadge rose too. "You might say it ruined yours. But your wife didn't read those books, Mr. Bayles. She didn't leave you because you locked a door. She ran for her life because although she couldn't put a name to it, she knew what you were."

The other stumbled forward, but Nordhall restrained him. "Now we've been very nice, Bayles; because this is Mr. Gamadge's pinch, and he likes things that way. But combat fatigue or not, I personally hope you'll get the works."

Bayles's head drooped again. He said: "I've had them."

"All right, now tell us about that boy Jerome Austen killed, before he hauls you into it."

"I didn't know a thing. He was a kid that used to do orderly work and chores in the hospital after school hours; they could use anybody. He thought Gray was a big hero, and Gray used to tell him to look the family up in New York. That's all."

"So it wasn't blackmail, just a boy looking for a break?"

Bayles looked from one to the other of them wildly. "I didn't know till afterwards; they didn't dare tell me. But *you* won't believe it." His eyes on Gamadge's, he clenched his hands.

Gamadge said: "I'm going on the stand to swear to it."

Bayles was silent. Then he said, half-whispering: "I never had a break myself till Gray Austen died."

Nordhall took him by the elbow. "All right, we'll be going downtown to get this in shape. Just give the sergeant your check stub, and he'll get your bag for you."

Gamadge watched them go; then he found a telephone booth and called the Malcolm apartment.

"Hello, Dave," he said. "Tell Mrs. M. that she won't have to give Serena a sleeping potion tonight. Gray Austen's stand-in tried to leave, and he's been nabbed, and he's told all. He's only too anxious to rat on the others, and he must have hated the very sight of them. Tell Serena the mystery of her marriage and of the former marriage is now made clear; he couldn't go out for diversion, so he was allowed it in the home. Nothing personal. The other poor girl probably died of a broken heart as much as anything."

"What's his name?" asked Malcolm. "Rena ought to know that, only decent."

"Bayles."

"I hope he killed Austen?" said Malcolm.

"No, we can't even pin that on him. Meningitis. Tell Serena that her trip wasn't wasted, even if we didn't need his lotions and medicine bottles after all. She threw such a scare into him with that line we gave her about scandal, and you fit to break down the door to get your sitter back, that he left at least twelve hours early; or so I imagine. That gets him away from the others, and we can move in on them to-morrow and they won't be expecting a thing."

"Fine. But now—"

"That's all for to-night. I want to go home."

"Yes, but how about those little books, and how you knew what was in them, and damn it, what they were?"

"It's a tale for a long winter's evening."

Gamadge hung up on Malcolm, found a cab, and went home. When he got there he was pardonably annoyed to find Mr. Norris Ordway settled at canasta with Clara in the library, and enjoying a light collation of cheese-on-toast and beer.

Ordway, rising, gave him a welcoming smile.

"Don't think of getting up," said Gamadge, dropping at full length on the chesterfield.

Ordway kindly brought him some beer. "I just dropped in," he said.

"I know. Your grandma happened to look out of the window and saw Miss Brown going into the Austen house and then coming out again, and probably she saw the police car go through afterwards. She wants the news."

"Dad says he's going to get her a night glass," said Ordway with quiet dignity.

Gamadge twisted around to look up at him. "You know, Mr. Ordway, I could get to like you a good deal."

"No trouble at all," remarked Clara.

"And I mean," continued Ordway, returning to his place at the card table, "I came here because you seemed to think that—Malcolm seemed to think—"

"Tell him not to worry at all. You can spend the day there to-morrow," said Gamadge, "you and the big dog can take out squatters' rights in the lobby."

"That means—" it was Clara's turn to rise.

"Yes, there won't be any counter-charges by Mr. Bayles, alias Austen. There won't be any divorce, unless I'm much mistaken. All right, all right, here we go."

But Gamadge couldn't be persuaded to tell about the little books. "I like to have everything under my eye and in cold print," he said, "where books are concerned. You'll have to wait, but it won't be long."

CHAPTER THIRTEEN

Cosy

ON MONDAY AFTERNOON, April the seventeenth, Jerome Austen and his sister were having their tea beside the window with the medallions of German stained glass. Norah, her face wreathed in smiles, passed plates of delicate little sandwiches. Aby sat under the table, rising to scraps and morsels as a trout rises to a fly.

Jerome nodded to Norah, speechless for the moment; then he got his sandwich down and said: "Tell her they're fine."

"Yes, sir, she knew you'd like them."

When Norah had gone Jerome said: "It's a relief, having that surly little brute out of the place."

"Yes, it's cosy. If it weren't for the risk..."

"No risk. Without the brace he'll be as spry as a cricket," said Jerome.

"I think it's so awful, having to pay him so much of our money," complained Hildreth. "How are you going to manage about forwarding money to him? The trustees mustn't know where he goes."

"My dear girl, I've had Gray's power of attorney since before the war."

"That's good. I think it was so silly of him to fly off like this in advance. Really he has no more nerve than poor Aby."

"He got on my nerves, all right. And out there when Gray died—why, when I put the thing up to him he jumped at it. Well, we're stuck with him, he's what we have to pay. And the worst of it is," said Jerome, laughing, "we can't even kill him; can't even wish him dead! Unless he has the decency to drown himself in mid-ocean. Forget him, he's gone."

"Was he absolutely sure that that boy had nobody to enquire after him, Jerry?"

"Yes, sure; the kid was a foundling, and I asked him myself whether he'd taken a job anywhere between this and California. It's all right, Hil, just remember that all that was far away and a long time ago."

"Well, you're a genius," said Hildreth. "Getting Tom to consult the Gamadge man, for instance; all *he* could do was to tell us to go to the Missing Persons place. And now if Wolfram asks, or the servants talk, we'll be all right. We had an expert in. Where did that book of his ever come from, I wonder? It's quite new—I mean it came out long after Uncle died."

"Where does a book come from? It's a Cresson book; Rena may have had it given her as a perquisite."

"Did you find out who those Malcolms are?"

"Yes, he's some kind of a writer all right. It's not so funny, their taking her in; people will do anything for extra help these days."

"Oh, how fortunate we were."

"Fortunate to get rid of Tommy Bayles and his moods and his marriages. It was on the cards to humour him a little, but good Lord what types he picked."

"He didn't have much choice," said Miss Austen, stretching back comfortably in her deep chair. "Took a lot of elimination to get just the right girls, and then how they turned out after all!"

"My dear child, they fell in love with him."

"Well, thank goodness that's over with."

The doorbell rang, and Aby whined.

"Still misses her," said Hildreth.

"Just so she hasn't come back for the rest of her clothes! I suppose we'll have to send them on eventually. Will you—"

"Oh, of course I will."

They relaxed, but after a minute she asked, looking towards the ante-room: "I wonder who that can be? Why doesn't Norah—"

Five people came directly into the library from the hall; a big weathered-looking man in a pin-stripe suit, a well-dressed business-man type, and three in uniform—two men and a woman. These last waited just inside the doors; the two others came forward. Aby barked once, half-heartedly, confused by numbers.

"Jerome Austen and Hildreth Austen," the big man said, "I am an officer of the law, and this gentleman is from the district attorney's office. I have a warrant here for your arrest, and the charge at present is conspiracy with one Thomas Bayles to defraud the heirs of the Charles Gray Austen estate, and embezzlement of the estate funds over a period of three years and ten months. Bayles—"

Jerome had got to his feet; he was holding himself erect by gripping the back of his chair. His thick jaws were sagging. Hildreth, crouching back as if to hide herself, had begun a thin screaming. Aby, from behind her chair, made a faint sound and was still.

"That little rat—" Jerome's voice was only half audible.

"He couldn't very well help himself, Austen," said the big man. "We took the brace off him and x-rayed his knee; and he's walking around as lively as anybody. Now we don't want any trouble at all. His squadron commander got in this morning, Gray Austen's is on the way, and we have all the proof we need of the impersonation without them or the rest of the evidence. We have a policewoman here to go up and help your sister get ready, and two men to do the same by you."

The policewoman came up and helped Hildreth Austen to her feet.

Gamadge, Lieutenant Nordhall and Sergeant Ryder had watched proceedings from a distance; they were grouped modestly in the drawing-room, whence they had a good view of the procession up the stairs. Norah was watching it too; she had come up from the basement to stand swaying against the banisters, her face yellowish in the dim light.

Nordhall addressed his companions briskly: "So that's that. Now we'd better get busy on the capital charge, and no time to waste. Here, you, Miss What's-your-name—Callahan."

The three walked along the hall to her. She had her eyes tight shut, her mouth had all but disappeared; she was shaking her head violently.

"Just answer some questions," said Nordhall.

"I don't know a thing." Norah opened her mouth to say this, but didn't open her eyes.

"If you've been listening, you know that Gray Austen has been in his grave four years, and this fellow Bayles was an impostor, and the other two were in it with him."

"I won't say one word."

"You seem to be on their side still. You'll be lucky if nobody suggests you were in it yourself."

"Me!" She was looking at him now. "Don't you dare say that," she squeaked.

"Kind of a hostile witness you'd be in court. Can't get it through your head that these people never had any right to the money, and won't have a cent now."

"That's for Mr. Dabney to tell me."

"You think your duty's to these crooks?" asked Nordhall. "Your duty is to old Mr. Austen and his estate. But if you're still sticking to the other side, it's not for me to make you say anything."

Gamadge said: "You know, Norah, you're a poor picker. The lady you knew as Mrs. Austen was the lady of this house in every sense of the word; but although you, with your experience, must have realized that very well, you chose to ingratiate yourself with the others, who didn't care about her, by treating her shabbily. She doesn't say so: I know what your attitude was at first hand."

Norah said in a low, angry voice: "She was the man's wife and had no right to leave him."

"You seem to know the rules," said Nordhall.

"Now," continued Gamadge, "you're carrying this dislike of her to the point of refusing to answer questions about these two Austens, who had no more right, as Lieutenant Nordhall says, to this money than you have."

"Whereas," said Nordhall, "if you did know anything that might help us with the case, it would put you right outside it."

Norah looked up at Gamadge. "You're a decent sort of man," she said, "and a gentleman. You know what I'd be like. You know anybody like me, that kept the same place thirty years, a place like this, wouldn't be in it with thieves."

"Then don't fight justice on their account," said Nordhall.

"I'd help you if I could. It's dazed I am."

"That's the way to talk," said Nordhall. "Let's go down to the basement—that's the place we're interested in."

Norah, mentally incapable by this time of asking him why, or of caring, went in front of them down the dark basement stairs.

CHAPTER FOURTEEN

Out of Place, Out of Time

"WE SOUND LIKE a herd of elephants," said Gamadge.

"I'll say we do." Nordhall eyed him quizzically through the dusk.

"It's one thing the old gentleman never did," said Norah, descending by putting both feet on each step each time, and holding to the banisters. "When the old carpet wore out he wouldn't renew. 'Leave it for our lifetime, Norah,' he'd say; he thought in those days he'd be willing the house to people that would only sell it or pull it down. Those institutions. 'I'll break my neck,' I'd tell him."

They went into one of those long basement rooms with a barred window and wainscoting, the kind of room that New Yorkers of moderate income used to take their meals in. It now contained a covered pool table, markers, and a rack of cues. Against the end wall stood an obsolete marble-topped sideboard in light oak, with glasses and bottles on its upper shelves and cupboards below. Sergeant Ryder leaned against one end of this, and took out a notebook. Nordhall faced his witness in the light from the window; Gamadge sat on the broad window-seat, looking out across the area at the basement gate.

"Now let's see," said Nordhall. "We understand from a member of the family that this was the place where all the liquor was, and that you got the cocktails ready down here every day."

"I had the keys to everything," said Norah. "I was in charge of this place, and you might say I was in charge of the house."

"Naturally you were. And cocktails were served by you in the library at half-past six, unless the family were playing pool down here."

"They'd drop in here for an extra drink when they felt like it, besides. But they preferred their cocktails up in the library, as a general thing."

"And you used these basement stairs."

"It was easier for me to be out of the kitchen and pantry, and away from the dining-room at that hour. The other girl would be setting the table for dinner."

"So you had all the fixings in here." Nordhall's eyes wandered to the sideboard.

"Yes, and I'd get the canapés from the cook." She added: "And the ice."

"Lots of work, getting all that ready."

"Eat like pigs, they did."

"Eat like pigs." Nordhall repeated it with a glance at her and at Gamadge that showed something besides satisfaction. Norah had put it all behind her, very natural.

"You'd be in here doing all this by six o'clock, would you?" he asked, watching her as he stood propped against the wall.

"Half an hour would give me plenty of time."

"You wouldn't be in here fixing cocktails a little earlier?"

"No, I would not."

"I thought you wouldn't." Nordhall sighed. "Now I'd like you just to cast your mind back to Saturday afternoon, Miss Callahan."

"One day was like another in this house."

"Oh, not lately," protested Nordhall, smiling at her. "You can't say that, can you? On Friday, late on Friday afternoon, for instance—the lady we'll call Mrs. Gray Austen ran away. That wasn't usual."

Norah's mouth puckered.

"And the gentleman we'll call Mr. Gray Austen," observed Gamadge, "got rid of a couple of books."

"And that wasn't usual," said Nordhall, "especially if he burned them."

The two waited; then Norah came through obligingly: "He put them on the library fire, and I found one charred up in the ashes and the other one all gone but the cover; a cover like that won't burn like paper and kindling wood. I had to put a log on top of it and crush it down."

"So they're all burned up now."

"Indeed they are; burned to ashes. And the ashes thrown in the garbage and taken away."

"Taken away. Then Saturday, Miss Callahan—you had a caller, Mr. Gamadge here. Now that wasn't usual either, was it?"

Norah gave Gamadge a quick apprehensive look. "We didn't have many, that's true."

"Naturally," said Nordhall, "because somebody might just happen to get a look at Mr. Gray Austen and wonder why he wasn't Mr. Gray Austen at all, but Thomas Bayles of Edgewood, Illinois."

She eyed him sourly.

"Well, Mr. Gamadge came," Nordhall went on, "and the three of them took him up to the second-floor sitting-room. Now"—and his voice changed, as it always did, Gamadge

noted with amusement, when he left facts for probabilities—
"at a little before six Jerome Austen left them, and went out of
the house. But Mr. Gamadge says he didn't hear the front door
slam after him, which is a sound that goes pretty well over the
house." He paused, and then said quietly: "So he must have
gone out by the basement way—door and gate."

Norah said nothing.

"But you weren't here at that time," conceded Nordhall.
"So we're interested in when and how he got home. It would
have been between six-fifteen and six-thirty, or so we figure
it, because Mr. Gamadge and Miss Austen left just before six-
fifteen and passed along the block towards the corner, and
Jerome Austen, for reasons of his own, wouldn't care to meet
Mr. Gamadge again just at that time."

"And how would the man know they'd come out then?"
asked Norah nastily.

"Well, he'd have to watch for them."

Norah, wrenching at her apron as if to wrench her mind
along these lines, said nothing.

"So you might have noticed him come in," said Nordhall.

"He never left the basement door open all that time, I'd
have felt the draught. He could have gone the other way and
used his front-door key."

"He could," agreed Nordhall gloomily.

"I was back and forth getting the canapés," said Norah. "I
never saw or heard him come into the house at all."

"Well, that's that then."

Norah gave him an evil smile. "But if you didn't think you
knew it all," she informed him, "and let me get a word in, I'd
have told you that I heard him go."

Gamadge burst out laughing. "Good for you, Norah; you'll
have the courtroom holding their sides, and the opposing coun-
sel's ears red. You weren't fixing cocktails, but you were here in
the basement before six o'clock just the same."

"And well before," she said triumphantly. "On Saturday
the groceries are always late. I was opening me olives and me

onions, and I was checking up on the liquor for the weekend. I might have had to run out for something."

"And you heard him come down those basement stairs."

"I did. Who else would it be in this house? And I heard the gate close behind him."

"But you didn't actually see him."

"No, I was back there at the buffet, with me back to the window. I thought he was coming in here, first; to get a drop, something extra before I had the tray ready. Or he might be going to practise up on his pool. Then when I heard him go past, and the gate crash to, I thought he'd gone first to mail a letter. Then I went back to the kitchen and thought no more of it, and at half-past six there he was up in the library, all ready for the cocktails."

"Well." Gamadge rose. "It's a big help, Norah—I mean it's a lot better than nothing. Don't bother your mind with it now, the sergeant has got it all down and I'm sure you'll remember it later."

Norah's mind had been working, slowly but steadily. She asked, looking from him to Nordhall: "Is it something else?"

"Well, yes, but—"

"Why would Jerome Austen be watching, afraid to meet anybody going home?... That felly was killed around the corner on Saturday." She stood biting her knuckles; her little eyes had an inward look. Then as Gamadge suddenly turned to the window, with Nordhall beside him, she came and peered out too.

A big car was at the kerb, with two smaller ones behind it; something of a crowd came down the steps of the house. There was a hunched female figure, wrapped in furs, with the policewoman helping her; there was a man, escorted by two officers—Gamadge would hardly have known him for Jerome Austen. He hung back a little, his face was bluish-grey and shining, his hat wouldn't stay on his head, but fell off twice, exposing ruffled hair. He stumbled getting into the car.

Nordhall said: "Bayles took his shock better than these people do."

"He hadn't so much on his mind."

Norah asked faintly: "Am I still in charge of the house?"

"Certainly you are," Nordhall assured her. "Mr. Dabney will be along any time to consult with you, and of course we'll want to know your immediate plans. Mustn't lose touch with us."

The other officials had got into their cars, and had driven away. Gamadge and Nordhall, with the sergeant faithfully at their heels, left the basement and went out into the street by the area gate.

"Well, I suppose we'd better go on from here," said Nordhall, standing with the others on the kerb. "Have yourself a cigarette, Ryder, it's the last you'll get for one while."

"You don't seem pleased," remarked Gamadge.

"Pleased? That's a hostile witness if ever I saw one. She nearly dished us in there, just from spite, and she'll do it again as soon as she gets a chance to. Say what you like to her, she's always going to think of Bayles's wife as Mrs. Gray Austen, and she's always going to hate her for being right about him; that Callahan type can't bear being in the wrong."

"That Callahan type goes where the money is," answered Gamadge. "Dabney's the one she'll want to please now—he's in charge of disbursements."

"Well, let's hope you're right about it. As for *this* idea of yours..." Nordhall shook his head. "If we don't get thrown out right away we'll have every obstacle there is laid out for us, and if we climb over those we won't get anywhere anyhow."

Ryder put in a word: "You haven't done as much of the routine stuff as we have, Mr. Gamadge. You don't know what it's like."

"I'm rather looking forward to it."

"All right," said Nordhall, casting his cigarette into the gutter, "come on then."

They crossed the street, walked up the block a way, and mounted steps to a handsome modern door. When it was opened by a pleasant-looking maid, Gamadge asked for Mr. Franklin Ordway.

"Yes, sir." She took his card.

"And two gentlemen from the Homicide bureau."

"Yes, sir." The maid looked startled, but ushered them into a drawing-room done up in chintzes of strong yellow and with a Chinese rug on the floor.

"This is the way to treat a north room," said Gamadge admiringly.

The maid came back and passed them through into a study which was all old carved oak and bottle-green velvet. The two men in the room were standing beside a great desk at which they seemed to have been working on papers. Ordway Senior was like his son in weight and colouring, but his short moustache and thick hair were getting grey. He watched the three come in with interest.

"Mr. Gamadge? Norris says you're a valued friend."

Norris Ordway's face had its usual expression of rock-like calm. He raised his hand in a half-salute to Gamadge.

"Very kind of him, Mr. Ordway," said Gamadge. "This is Detective-lieutenant Nordhall; and this is Sergeant Ryder."

Ordway said: "Sit down, won't you? Norris, why don't you hand cigarettes?"

"Thanks, have my own." Nordhall, subsiding gently into a green-velvet armchair, took over: "It's a kind of a delicate job we're on, Mr. Ordway. You may not like the idea."

"Have to like it if you do," said Ordway cheerfully.

"That don't always follow, wish it did," said Nordhall. "I'll get right down to it. You know there was a murder up here on Madison couple of days ago—Saturday afternoon."

"So I saw in the papers."

"Mr. Gamadge seems to have got hold of the idea somehow that your mother might have seen something out of her window that might have some value for us in our investigation," said Nordhall doggedly.

Ordway, sitting behind his desk and smoking his pipe with all his offspring's calm, turned his head to look at Norris gravely.

"I admit," he said, moving his eyes back to Nordhall, "that my mother doesn't miss much of what's going on in the block; she can't get about as she would like, and it's an interest for her. But I hardly think she witnessed a murder. She'd have mentioned it. Wouldn't she, Norris? Or would she?"

Norris said: "She was quite interested in this affair, Dad. Saw the excitement. Sent me out for news, in fact, and I met Mr. Gamadge at the scene of the crime. I think he has a kind of a cult for Gram."

"I have," said Gamadge.

"So we thought," continued Nordhall, "that she might just possibly have seen somebody we're interested in coming or going; as we need evidence of any kind whatsoever, hers would be—"

"Oh." Ordway pondered. "Well, it's quite possible. Do you want us to ask her? She's a very old lady, and she couldn't by any means appear in court, you know, hang around as a witness. That would be out of the question."

"Never thought of such a thing. A sworn statement," said Nordhall. "The D.A.'s office would take care of it. But we'd like to see her ourselves, if it was convenient. And without any kind of preparation, if you understand what I mean."

Ordway thought this over. Then he looked at his son and smiled. "Think she'd enjoy it?"

"Very much," said Norris.

"All right, come along. You'll permit us to be present, I hope?" He rose, still smiling, and they all rose.

"More witnesses, the better we like it."

"Good."

Five men, all of them tall and four of them large, went up two flights of stairs in single file.

"Old lady climb these?" panted Nordhall.

Ordway looked over his shoulder at him. "Oh yes; three times a day. Born to it."

They arrived at the third floor landing; Ordway went along to a front room, looked in, and said: "Some gentlemen to see you, Mother; business."

A clear old voice said: "Bring them in, dear, bring them in."

They went in to a big cheerful bedroom, where an old lady sat in a window with a big dog at her feet. The dog raised his head, stared, and then slowly laid his muzzle down again on his paws. The old lady raised *her* head, looked at the invading horde with surprise, and adjusted her spectacles. Her face had a slightly aquiline cast, and her features were firm but benign.

"I hope there are chairs," she said.

Norris performed the introductions. When he came to Gamadge she smiled. "I've been hoping to meet you," she said, "and your wife—and your guest."

"Paying guest, I assure you."

Everybody sat down except Ordway Senior, who said he would stay at the door to keep the gate. "Servants always popping in to see how Mother's getting on."

Nordhall, opposite her, asked her kindly to throw her mind back as far as Saturday afternoon.

Mrs. Ordway obediently assumed a thoughtful look.

"There was some trouble around the corner," he reminded her. "A little before half-past six. You noticed the excitement, I understand; from your window here. Now would you have noticed any comings and goings to and from the Austen house in the preceding three quarters of an hour? Say between a quarter to six and the time the crowd began to gather?"

Mrs. Ordway said amiably: "I don't keep looking out of the window all the time, you know. I glance out now and then."

"Certainly, we understand that," said Nordhall.

"I happened to glance out some little time after six o'clock, and I saw this Mr. Gamadge come down the steps with the Miss Austen who lives there with her brothers."

"Gram," said Norris, "you're 'way behind the times. Haven't you taken a gander out all this afternoon?"

"If anything was going on, Norris, you might have told me."

"Dad thought it was too rugged for you."

Nordhall brought the conversation back to where it had been broken off: "But earlier, Mrs. Ordway? Less than half an hour earlier?"

"I didn't happen to look earlier. No."

Nordhall sat back, disconsolately dragging his hands along his thighs. "Well," he said, "I suppose it was too much to expect."

"I'm very sorry to disappoint you, Lieutenant."

"But perhaps you went on looking after Mr. Gamadge and Miss Austen passed—with the little dog?" He sat forward again. "See anybody go back in?"

Sergeant Ryder had his notebook open on his knee, pencil poised; Ordway Senior was leaning against the doorjamb, looking amused; Norris Ordway and Gamadge, about to light the cigarettes which Norris had produced, sat intent and motionless, Norris with his lighter in his hand; Mrs. Ordway had leaned her head back against the cushions of her chair, taken off her spectacles, and closed her eyes. Nordhall's icy blue ones were fixed on her quiet face.

Presently she raised her lids, returned Nordhall's piercing look with one of mild clarity, and said: "Yes. I saw him going up the steps soon after Mr. Gamadge and his sister and the little dog went by. I was looking after them, and then I looked back and saw him go up the steps."

"Saw who, ma'am?" Nordhall was again gripping his knees.

"Mr. Austen. The lame man."

Nordhall's expression was so blank, the silence in the room so intense, that she felt a need to apologize: "I've said the wrong thing? I can't help it, Lieutenant; it was the lame one. Even if he hadn't been helping himself up by the railing, I know that coat and hat."

Nordhall and Gamadge, eyeing each other, suddenly smiled; Ryder burst into uncontrollable laughter, and slapped his knee. Mrs. Ordway, surprised, raised her eyebrows at him, and he stiffened to official gravity.

"Excuse us, Mrs. Ordway," said Nordhall, getting hold of himself. "No way to behave, it's no laughing matter. But you gave us a surprise. We seem to be having a little trouble this afternoon with places and times. The lame man, as you call him, and you certainly are behind the times, was still in the house—Mr. Gamadge had left him up on the third floor, and he couldn't have come out until after Gamadge and Miss Austen did, and so he couldn't have made it. Not even with his brace off."

"Brace off?"

"And he won't like it when he hears that Jerome Austen borrowed his limp and his outdoor things to commit a murder in."

Mrs. Ordway replaced her spectacles to gaze at him.

Nordhall turned to Gamadge: "He didn't worry about Norah seeing him, he forgot that the groceries come late on Saturday afternoon. Ran down those basement stairs and out the gate. But he wasn't taking any chances outdoors. So far as he knew, nobody was ever going to connect any of the Austens with this murder; but he might be noticed around the entrance to that service alley down the street, and—well, you see the beauty of it. No lame man would think of attempting a murder like that; he wouldn't risk it—not the kind of lame man that one push could shove off balance or even off his feet."

"Dark evening," said Gamadge. "And with that soft hat turned down, and his collar up—and they were much of a height, and the same colouring. Bayles implied, you remember, that a casual description would fit either him or Gray Austen; it might fit him and Gray Austen's brother, I suppose, if you didn't look too closely. I saw them together; I think Jerome could get away with it in the circumstances. In fact, so far as Mrs. Ordway was concerned, he did."

Mrs. Ordway spoke, rather loudly for her: "Are you saying that that child's husband wasn't lame, and wasn't Gray Austen at all?"

Nordhall rose. "Perhaps Mr. Gamadge would stay a while and explain. The sergeant and I have got to run. You've done us a big favour, ma'am; now if you'll let some people come up and take your sworn statement…"

"Delighted. I know these two relatives of mine won't let me go to court, but I don't see why I—"

Mr. Ordway said: "Out of the question, as you know." Shaking hands with Nordhall, he remarked that things seemed to be getting a little lively on this quiet residential block. "My son and I witnessed a most extraordinary sight when we were getting home just now; it almost looked as if the two elder Austens—I hardly know them by sight myself—had to be forcibly removed from their premises by police."

"That's so, sir. Mr. Gamadge will tell you all about it. It's his pinch, you know."

Ordway glanced at Gamadge with politely restrained astonishment.

"Just some evidence I happened to run into," said Gamadge. "I'm not police myself."

"At present the charge is only fraud and embezzlement," Nordhall went on regretfully.

"Trifle, of course." Ordway's expression was blank.

"But we hope to get this murder charge to stick. We have the evidence of the accomplice, this Bayles who was posing as Gray Austen, but we'd like some corroboration, and I think we're getting it."

"I see you are. Well. I confess I'm astounded. The father was a bad hat, I believe, something wrong about money. But I hardly imagined that that branch of the family had gone so completely off the rails."

"We'll piece it out sooner or later."

He and Ryder took their leave, refusing to be seen down to the front door. When they had gone Mrs. Ordway addressed her grandson; her eyes were glittering:

"Norris?"

"Gram?"

"I think in the circumstances we might tell your father now."

"If Mr. Gamadge says so."

"All right with me," said Gamadge.

"Tell me what?" Ordway Senior looked from one to the other of his relatives, suspicion in his eye. "And why now? Why not at first, whatever it is?"

"We thought it might be too rugged for you," said his son paternally.

CHAPTER FIFTEEN

The Wrong Crime

MORNING SUNLIGHT WAS finding its way through the leaden panes of the northeast window in the Austen library; Gamadge, having arrived by appointment, was sent in unannounced by a Norah whose face had sagged into what looked like permanent lines of chagrin. He stood at the doorway looking at Rena and Mr. Dabney, who sat at the centre table over lists.

Rena saw him, got up and came to him, reached her arms around his neck and kissed him.

"My orphan." Gamadge returned to the table with her, arm in arm. Mr. Dabney smiled in approbation.

"This is Mr. Gamadge, Mr. Dabney. He—"

"I know." They shook hands.

"Literature brought the young person and myself together," said Gamadge. "Books, if not literature, unite us still." He laid a flat package on the table and began to take off the string.

"So I am given to understand," said Dabney, "and I am deeply interested."

"I thought you might be." Gamadge took the paper off his parcel, disclosing an old book catalogue; he said: "And since you have been so kind to our friend here…"

Mr. Dabney was a tired-looking little old man, but he had plenty of professional authority left in manner as well as in voice. "My dear sir!" he exclaimed. "'Kind'? This lady has been victimized. So has the Austen estate, which I think I understand you to have rescued in a most spectacular—"

"Just chance."

"Very well. You rescued it; but for you we might have lost fifty years of income. As it is, we have only lost three years and ten months of income, and in fact not all of that. Bayles at least had saved something, which will be restored to us in due time. But this lady—we can't compensate *her*. I don't call her small effects, her clothing and some articles of jewelry, adequate compensation. And yet she insists that this inventory she has made must go to the appraisers, and that she can't take the stuff out of the house. Really! I have discretionary powers."

"If you can't bear the sight of the things, Serena," said Gamadge, "sell them and put the money towards your law costs."

"That, indeed," said Mr. Dabney, "would be poetic justice." She said: "I could do that."

"And if you have discretionary powers, Mr. Dabney," Gamadge went on, "I hope to goodness you'll put a value on the books upstairs in the sitting-room and let me buy the lot."

"The bank will certainly agree with me that if you are willing to accept any such inadequate fee—"

"I accept it," said Gamadge eagerly.

"Then that's settled." Mr. Dabney made a note. "You will receive them carriage prepaid. As for our responsibility"—he sighed heavily—"I don't know. But concerning forgeries, we could only think of him as his own verification, with the Austen family behind him."

"And with Gray Austen behind him, out west."

"So I hear. A strange outgrowth, all this, from a decent old New York family. Rackets, I understand, and the woman had lost her position in that library for some extraordinary reason connected with morals."

"Bayles came of a good New England family," said Gamadge, "settled in Illinois. He was a misery to his relations from the day he was old enough to shirk a job and lie himself out of the consequences. The air force was the only outfit he ever made good in, and he quit when he could—too much work there, as he freely says. I suppose he and Gray Austen were natural affinities. But you're not the only girl who fell in love with him, Serena; he had plenty of charm, it wasn't all your imaginative sympathy."

"He seemed so sad and lost."

"He was. That brace of Austen's did it; it caught you, but it had caught him. He says now that the only profession he could have followed with any pleasure was acting, and the war did him out of it."

"I should say he had exercised his abilities to the full in private life," remarked Mr. Dabney. "That poor boy Pedersen, who came on to see his hero again and couldn't be allowed to hang about for the purpose—will these people manage to involve Bayles in that crime?"

"No, they can't. Apart from my testimony, there's Jerome's impersonation of him when he committed the murder. Nobody could possibly think that Bayles would like that, but it was a necessary part of the plan from the start. He was accessory after the fact, of course, against which the police have his voluntary statement, made not much more than twenty-four hours later."

"And when," asked Mr. Dabney, his eyes on the catalogue in Gamadge's hands, "are we to have that statement from you?"

"I haven't made it to anybody else," said Gamadge, "you're the first to hear it." He looked at Serena and smiled. "Two thin books, much of a size: one a report of a trial, the other the judge's summing-up; they were fastened together, you know, they belonged to each other. And the summing-up was printed in two columns in fine type—plenty of reading matter there."

Mr. Dabney wrinkled up his forehead, and Gamadge laughed.

"I was puzzled too," he said.

"Yes, it puzzles me; but I can't quite—"

"Nor could I. And I couldn't even decide *what* was puzzling me. Because of the old books only one of them seemed to stir a memory, and that one wasn't the trial but the other. And it wasn't so much what was in the other, as what its format was. That's as near as I could get."

Mr. Dabney, his eyes fastened on Gamadge, shook his head.

"Until a week ago yesterday," said Gamadge, "when Miss Austen honoured me by calling. Quite naturally, they all wanted to know how the police were getting along with their investigation of the murder, and wanted also to know how hard the police might work on it. She lamented the vulgarity of the press, she said that if the boy had been important there would have been columns and columns about him; and added (her mind on hazardous publicity): 'Far too much.'

"*They do far too much*, was her thought. But what registered itself in my brain was first the columns and columns of fine print in that summing-up, and then the thought that compared with the trial, any trial, the summing-up was too long; far too long, longer than—"

Mr. Dabney put up a hand: "Wait. No. Yes. No."

"Well, you're a lawyer," said Gamadge, "but this case was tried, and *another* case was tried and summed up, many years ago. I'm a book man in an amateur kind of way; I see and handle and read about all kinds of books, and my interest in trials is you might say a reader's interest. Miss Austen unlocked a compartment in my brain which held the memory of the longest summing-up in legal history. There was a celebrated case—only it wasn't a murder case; there was as a result a trial for perjury; and the summing-up of that trial—"

Mr. Dabney stood entranced; he said in a wondering voice: "No wonder Bayles didn't care who read what murder cases!"

"And no wonder I went wrong," said Gamadge, "with all those murder cases and trials and crime novels in the book shelves."

Rena asked: "Not a murder case?"

"No. Here you are."

She leaned over to read the item aloud:

TICHBORNE CASE

The Summing-up of the Lord Chief Justice, together with the Addresses of the Judges, the Verdict, and the Sentence, in the Trial of Arthur Orton, Claimant, for Perjury. Accompanied by a history of the Tichborne Case, and a copious index.

8vo, half morocco. London, 1874

"That was the bound book," Gamadge told her. "The other book, the Tichborne Trial itself, was the case involving a fraudulent claim to an estate. The Claimant lost, and was then tried for perjury; as he never got his hands on any of the estate funds, he couldn't be tried for embezzlement.

"You remember when we talked about forming a company, Rena, to pay for your divorce suit? That rang a bell; the Claimant, Orton, had a bunch of stockholders behind him, backing him with their shillings and half-crowns, poor things."

"Another thing might have—ah—rung a bell," said Mr. Dabney, exhilarated by a chance to match Gamadge's historical information. "The main strength of the Claimant's case rested on the astounding fact that the lost heir's own mother recognized and accepted the pretender. Or thought she recognized him, or"—Mr. Dabney smiled—"pretended to do so. She didn't like the legal heirs. This fellow Bayles seemed to have family backing too."

"It rang no bell," admitted Gamadge. "What got to me at last was Miss Austen's reference to 'columns and columns,' coupled with her phrase: 'more than you'd expect.' Those little books, and Rena's description, had been in my mind for more than thirty-six hours, and—such is memory."

"I had it all in my hands on Friday afternoon," said Rena.

"We can now analyse the scene that took place on that Friday afternoon," said Gamadge. "We can follow it from beginning to end. The man had had a double shock when he gave you that murderous look; he was half out of his wits with terror when he locked that door. First he saw the report of the Tichborne trial in your hands, caught the title, and knew what it was. It's a very famous case, and has often been referred to and described in memoirs and collections. He may have read about it or only heard about it—but he knew it. At first, obsessed as he was—Jerome said so, you remember—he was sure you'd caught on to him." Gamadge paused. "I half think he may have had an excuse for jumping to that conclusion."

"I never—" began Rena.

"No, but his first wife may have found him out; wouldn't that explain her better than any explanation we thought of before? She couldn't bring herself to leave this man who turns out to be a criminal, and who doesn't even care for her. He treats her now as a potential danger to him, and so do the others treat her. They never let her alone. She's in it with them, too, and she's a simple not very well educated character who can't take it."

"So when I—"

"So he instantly jumps to his conclusion; but you persuade him that he has been wrong. He's calming down; and then what do you say? You say you want to leave him, that he doesn't really need you.

"What can he, in his state, think of that? He can only think that you mean he isn't really lame at all. He rushes out to consult his accomplices, and he locks you in.

"But then Jerome, who has more discernment than Bayles where people are concerned, laughs him out of it. You couldn't possibly carry such a suspicion, much less such knowledge, for a day without showing that you had it. Bayles must go up and let you out and apologize, before you get it into your head that something is very wrong with them all.

"But he finds that you have flown. So now, Jerome tells him, the thing is to behave as innocent people behave, but without running any risk of putting ex-Captain Gray Austen into the limelight. Consult a private man, and let him find her if he will—but of course he won't. Not the kind of private man this Gamadge seems to be."

A slight sound in the doorway made them all turn. Norah stood there, an obsequious smile on her face, Aby at her side.

"Excuse me, ma'am," she said, "and Mr. Dabney. We're all ready to go to-morrow. What's to become of *him*?"

Aby's frog face looked anxious; too many people had gone away, more were certainly going—he had observed trunks and bags; he didn't see his future clear. He gazed up at Rena diffidently.

"Poor little Aby," she said, "I'll take you."

CHAPTER SIXTEEN

To Be Answered

Dear Gamadge,

Annulment proceedings are under way, and there will be no difficulties. Bayles was guilty of felony before the marriage with Miss Seton, and during the whole term of the marriage, and in fact married her in the name of the man he was impersonating.

Let me have the address of this Mrs. Ordway she is staying with. I am glad she has found a friend to pay costs.

Well, you didn't actually have to kill the fellow. Congratulations on the short cut.

Yours
Robert Macloud

Henry Gamadge, Esq
Dear Mr. Gamadge,

I am informed by the lady we knew as Mrs. Gray Austen that I may address a letter to you as her next friend. I wish to explain that I of course never had occasion to examine Bayles's knee; that was a surgeon's job, or would have been. He had, and on one occasion showed me, all the x-ray reports and other records which Mr. Gray Austen had brought away with him from the military hospital in California.

Bayles wore Austen's bracelet with identification tag, and had all other papers of course. It is the most fantastic thing that has ever come into my experience.

I have wondered whether his first wife may not have found him out. It must have been very difficult for him to maintain the deception, but from his second wife's testimony we know that he was able to do so in her case. I feel very sorry about the first Mrs. Bayles. Once or twice I would have asked her whether she hadn't something on her mind, but I never saw her privately; she was much hedged in.

Very truly yours
Kurt Wolfram

Dear Mr. Gamadge,

It is lovely up here at the Ordways', and Mrs. Ordway wants me to say that I am taking good care of her. We read aloud, knit and do cross-stitch. It is not so quiet weekends, when Norris and Mr. Ordway come up, and later they will have vacations.

Gawain is so kind to Aby. He is showing him all over the place, and they hunt together. Just like that "steady brother" in our favourite song.

Norah wrote to me. She said she had heard on the block that Mrs. Ordway had "adopted" me, and didn't we need a personal maid who knew my ways and wouldn't rake up old stories. Mrs. Ordway answered for me, and won't tell me what she said.

I was glad to hear from Mr. Macloud. Pretty soon you will be able to call me Miss Seton again. It will make me feel better never to have been married.

Please give my love to everybody, and thank them all again. I will see you and Clara when I come in to keep my appointment with Mr. Macloud.

Don't forget me.

Rena

Dear Mr. Gamadge,

This is to assure you that all is well here and will be. When my grandson repeated to me (I confess with roars of laughter) the conversation you once had with him during which you implied a warning not to trifle with Rena's affections, I admit that I felt annoyance with you. But afterwards, realizing the delicacy of her position and your own sense of responsibility, I forgave you.

But I am still disappointed in you. Why, if at first sight you could recognize her qualities, could you not at first sight recognize my grandson's?

However, I am most grateful to you. We shall all be most discreet in the coming year, and we shall all be happy.

With kindest regards, I am

Sincerely yours
Malvina Ordway

P.S. That Boston terrier. Oh well, they tell me he is old.

Sadly, this was the last book in the "Henry Gamadge" series by Elizabeth Daly. If you're curious about other books in Felony & Mayhem's Vintage category, here are the first chapters of two of our other Vintage titles: *Mr Campion's Farthing*, by Philip Youngman-Carter, a mystery that continues Margery Allingham's "Albert Campion" series, written by her husband and originally published in 1969; and *My True Love Lies*, by Lenore Glen Offord, a mystery set in the San Francisco art world, originally published in 1947, and coming out from Felony & Mahem Press in January 2017.

MR CAMPION'S FARTHING

CHAPTER 1

Variation on a Theme

THE MAN WHO STOOD like a block of grey stone at the edge of a belt of elm trees was looking down a gentle slope towards his intended victim. For several minutes he had not moved, partly to make sure that he was quite alone but also because he was absorbed by the technical side of the problem.

There was the possibility of incidental death, which would be rated as murder, but this was no longer a deciding factor. He had already balanced risk again precaution, penalty against reward, and now after days of waiting the odds were in his favour.

The night wind was blowing in gusts from the South East, the perfect direction for his purpose. It made the evergreens in the garden below him chatter together; they and the outhouse doors nagging at their latches would conceal any betraying footfall.

To his left a bolster of cloud reflected the sodium street lights of London whose fringe began only five miles away and stretched for another forty. Below and ahead of him the motorway cut a deep swathe through the fields, proclaiming its presence by a procession of headlights which glowed and waned as they streamed eastwards to the coast.

The house, four hundred yards distant, presented its unlikely silhouette as each vehicle entered the arc of the by-pass, only to vanish as it drew level. In this theatrical lighting the black shape suggested a toy fort built for a giant's child or a Bavarian castle lifted from its mountain top by Disney for the entertainment of Londoners in the green belt which surrounds the city with half-urbanized grassland.

Inglewood Turrets has been described by cynics as a mongrel by St Pancras Station out of Holloway Gaol and this is not unjust. It is of whitish stucco, crenellated and illogical with occasional cones of steely slate projecting from assorted roofs. The walls are pierced by gothic windows, whose diamond panes, tormented by borders of coloured glass, dye the surrounding trees alternately heliotrope and puce. But the most remarkable thing about the house is that it should have survived for over ninety years.

At its creation it was hailed as 'Cambric's Folly', for Sir Edwin had disagreed with several architects and finished by drawing his own plans and getting, as he generally did, his own way. He was of Huguenot blood, a textile prince who saw only one side of the coin: that which showed his own image and superscription. He had immortal longings and did not recognize opposition.

At the Turrets he had entertained most of the intellectual lions of his day and many who came to scoff remained to prey upon his patronage. He was an excellent host who kept a fine cellar and understood the art of promoting and listening to good gossip.

Though he bought royally from academicians, in literary matters he was more discriminating and helped more than one poet from obscurity to fame. Nearly every celebrity of the age had enjoyed his friendship and his table. Some have even paid tribute in forgotten memoirs. There are many references to him in the *Greenaway Diaries*, the *Letters of Lord Mountfitchet*, and Mrs St John Gregory has described a Christmas week of the late '90s in nostalgic detail.

The host himself was painted by Millais, Solomon J. Solomon, Hubert von Herkomer and John Sargent, his whiskers changing from chestnut to white as canvas succeeded canvas over the baroque mantelpiece of Italian marble in the dining hall.

Sir Edwin may have been a pompous unimportant eccentric, as Mountfitchet, who survived his hospitality for twenty graceless years, observed; but he had a glorious time making an ass of himself, did no man harm, and enjoyed every moment of it.

Sir William Gilbert, who had often partnered him at golf, was deeply moved by his death, and Sir Arthur Sullivan's 'Lost Chord' was played as an organ voluntary at the memorial service. Royalty, in the person of a retired Major-General, was represented and Max Beerbohm shed an overt tear into his remarkable top hat.

In a sense the house died in 1904 along with its first master, but it was embalmed intact. Not a stick was sold; every picture, curtain, trophy and nicknack remained where the owner had decreed it should be placed, for Lucian his son was a professional soldier, a colonel in Prince Albert's Very Own, who preferred Poona and Polo to obsolescent culture. The gardens dwindled but remained trim, the furniture was polished and dusted, but much of the park land, including the private golf course, was sold to farmers and speculative builders. Commerce encroached on the Turrets but did not devour it. In later years enlightened legislators, though they made no preservation orders, forbade further development except for the by-pass which cut deep into the approach, destroying the rustic lodge, the ornamental lake and the wrought-iron gates.

The present owner, Miss Charlotte Cambric, a great-niece of Sir Edwin, had very clear ideas on the subject of running an expensive anachronism which was also a Victorian treasure house. It was her life and her livelihood.

The man watching the house was not concerned with history or aesthetics. He was making a final check before the first trespass.

His appearance was exactly as he intended it to be, totally unremarkable from his shapeless green felt hat to his grey suit and his rubber-soled shoes. The anonymity went deeper; not a tailor's label or a laundry mark remained to betray him and his brown gloves were designed to leave no print on anything he touched. An empty envelope picked up in the street and addressed to a total stranger was an insurance in case he was required to produce proof of identity. He carried an old army haversack slung over one shoulder and this, for the moment, was incriminating; but the contents were essential and he would soon be rid of them.

A square of light in one of the servants' rooms above the coach house, now the garage, died abruptly, leaving only three glimmering needles to mark the galleried chamber called the Music Room. He gave himself ten minutes by the mass-produced wrist-watch as impersonal as his muffler and began to walk deliberately down the hedge leading to the garden wall and the new approach which replaced the road wiped away by the by-pass. No point in behaving suspiciously: if he was questioned he was bringing a message for a non-existent chauffeur. Miss Cambric did not admit to owning a telephone.

He walked steadily down the tradesmen's drive, keeping to the grass verge by the laurels, and halted at last in the protection they offered. The moon looked unexpectedly through the scudding clouds and the final yards had to be made without cover. The entrance to the low-level courtyard lay beneath a gothic archway which suggested a portcullis. Once down the cobbled slope and into the lee of the walls and he would be safe. He crossed the open space in the moment of complete darkness which followed as the clouds closed in.

The situation was better than he had hoped, for a large American car, too long for its allotted space, squatted half-way between the open doors of a garage and at the back of this lay a door into the house itself. It was not secured, which meant that he had ten minutes in hand, valuable extra time to ensure perfection. In unbroken silence he reached the semi-basement level of the wood store which had apparently been designed as the interior of a wood-cutter's cottage for 'Hansel and Gretel'. He paused to unpack his haversack, pick out a torch and find the tools he needed to deal with the door to the wine cellar.

The lock presented no problem; it was decorated in tortured iron but had not been made to provide serious opposition to an intruder. It yielded without a creak and he found himself standing on the cool stone floor of the vault, cluttered with discarded crates and the straw wrappings of bottles which had been stacked in the racks lining the walls. Here the architecture suggested a dungeon—and, indeed, Sir Edwin had called the service lift beside the spiral staircase the Oubliette.

The intruder made six separate piles of logs, straw and broken boxes, constructing each with unhurried care. To each he added three small white square firelighters, and a sprinkling of paraffin from the bottle he had brought. The door at the top of the stone steps leading up to the ground floor was slightly ajar and he considered this carefully for a minute, calculating the flow of air. It would be wiser to close it and rely on the gratings at ground level to provide a through draught. The smoke must not get into the house before the oak beams of the ceiling were well ablaze, or the alarm might be given too soon. He pushed the latch home and wedged the foot of the frame with a wooden peg from a barrel.

If the big car, which might contain more than a dozen gallons of petrol, could be successfully fired, it would block the outer entrance and leave the centre of the house defenceless to burn as fiercely as an incinerator.

He made a final survey of his work, re-siting one of the heaps to ensure that the main wood stack could be caught on three sides, and as an afterthought dropped his haversack amongst the logs. Six matches and the job would be complete.

Half an hour after midnight: zero.

With a box in one hand and the first match in the other he froze, listening intently, aware of a trickle of sweat running down his neck from his hatband.

Far off in a room above him a woman was singing.

Back through sixty odd years came the plummy contralto of Madam Kirkby Lunn's recorded ghost, wailing faintly through the enormous brass horn of an instrument called a Senior Monarch Phonograph.

'He—e—e shall fe—e—e—ed his flock like a shepherd...'

Another sound, close behind him, came too swiftly for reaction, and the blow caught him off balance. He pitched head forward on to the flagstones into oblivion. The matches which had been in his hand spun in the air to fall in a cascade on his neck. The box rested for a moment on his shoulder and then slid to the ground.

The unbroken torch beside his body threw a long shaft of light on to the piles of kindling and the eddying dust.

The voice, faint as pot-pourri, flowed on.

'And he shall ga—a—ther the lambs...'

There was often music at the Turrets on a Sunday night.

MY TRUE LOVE LIES

(HAPTER 1

THIS WAS THE TWELFTH of September, six-thirty of a mild, overcast evening. On clear days about this time, San Francisco's tall buildings would reflect the level sunlight in a dazzle of windows, but tonight they rose into an atmosphere of veiled softness. A few blocks away the traffic of Market Street sent up a muted clatter and roar. The sidewalks around the Civic Center were alive with people hurrying home.

From where Noel Bruce sat at the wheel of a parked sedan, most of what met the eye was Navy, sailor collars, stone-gray summer uniforms and dress blues concentrated in front of the Twelfth Naval District building. It was the more remarkable, therefore, that at a distance of fifty feet Noel should be able to recognize one particular officer, whom she had met only once before.

She was a paid driver for the Navy. Since noon on this September day she had been transporting naval personnel about the city, returning after each call to the Twelfth Naval

District. At the end of her working day she still looked trim and her uniform was becoming, a fact brought home to her by the side glances of three ensigns standing and talking at the curb.

Noel put on what she hoped was an official look. She was not, however, thinking about the ensigns, but figuring that in about an hour she'd be through. It wouldn't leave her too much time to dress for the party at the Sherwin Art School, but she'd make it. She was going off into vague musings about what to wear when the man appeared in the doorway and stood glancing up and down the line of parked sedans and station wagons.

He came toward her car, with that long free stride and indefinable look of race that had caught her eye among all the other blue uniforms. There was a terrific snapping of salutes as he neared the ensigns on the sidewalk, and the three younger men melted away, for some reason looking abashed and startled. Lieutenant Miles Coree met Noel's eyes and gave her an odd, shy grin that belied his air of complete assurance.

"So it *is* you," he said, and folded his long frame into the seat beside her. "Luck's with me, for once! I asked for your ticket on the off chance you'd be free."

"Why, thank you," said Noel in a tone of sweet reserve. She glanced at the ticket and reached for the ignition.

"Wait a minute," the man said. "Will you let me tell you something? The other night, at the Servicemen's Art Center, I didn't have a chance to say goodbye to you. I've been regretting it ever since."

"And you want to say it now?" Noel inquired helpfully.

Lieutenant Coree made a sound between a groan and laughter. "Nothing of the sort. Do let me tell you, Miss Bruce. I thought I saw someone I knew looking in the doorway, and then turning to leave without coming in. I thought I'd catch my friend in the courtyard; no. Then I really put on steam, and got clear down Grant Avenue before I saw I was chasing the wrong person."

"Annoying."

"You do agree?" said the lieutenant with relief. "Thank Heaven for that; first sign of relenting. It seemed I couldn't go back. I was just too damned embarrassed, because I'd walked out on you, and I'm embarrassed now. But I've been trying to catch up with you ever since, and that makes two women I couldn't find. Could we wash out my bad manners and start again?"

She said, "Don't be embarrassed. I didn't mind a bit, I was just surprised."

Lieutenant Coree clicked his tongue and gave her a reproachful look. "And I thought of you languishing there with a broken heart. Well, well, I might have spared my conscience, but it's a blow to a man's vanity." He met her eye and grinned again, so ruefully and disarmingly that she dissolved in friendly laughter.

"And now," said Noel Bruce, "maybe we'd better get started on the Navy's business?"

Listening to his pleasant, easy conversation while she threaded the northbound traffic of Larkin Street, she thought: How queer that two of us should have been mistaken, last Friday night, about the person we saw in the studio doorway; I'd have sworn it was Tannehill, with her hand in a sling, but she told me she hadn't been there that evening. Double hallucination—does that make us soul mates, or something?

She was disproportionately pleased to see Miles Coree again, and to learn that he'd been looking for her.

An hour later, while she was waiting for him outside the Army docks at Fort Mason, she took stock of her feelings once more and found that a new element had crept in. It was as if that pin-prick of curiosity and annoyance from last Friday night had disappeared under a counter-irritant, for now, with no tangible reason, she was uneasy. It had nothing to do with Lieutenant

Coree, surely? It was only that each time she met him, something remotely puzzling occurred.

There was no reason why they shouldn't have made that brief side trip to the Plaster Works on their way to the docks, and it was natural enough that he should have suggested it after she'd been telling him about Sherwin, and her special friends who were sculptors. Nothing had actually happened there to disquiet her, unless you counted that unintelligible muttering from the crazy old watchman beyond the fence.

Noel turned to look behind her, but nothing untoward appeared in the grayly lighted street that flanked the docks. She noted with approval and some relief the presence of a stalwart pair of guards at the entrance. The illusion that someone was following her wasn't her style at all, and she turned back with determination to the official eyes-front position.

Lieutenant Coree, it seemed, was a radar technician. He was inspecting equipment on a ship which was due to sail in the morning. The inspection shouldn't take too long, he had told her, being considerate and anxious about her working overtime. At the moment that aspect seemed unimportant to Noel. She was quite frankly wondering if she would ever see Miles Coree again after this evening. His leave, he had said, would begin on Friday, the day after tomorrow. He was going back to St. Louis to see his parents.

"If I never do see him again," Noel told herself with a sudden chuckle, "I have a fine souvenir of the evening." She slid a small drawing pad from her uniform pocket and flipped over the half dozen sketches on its first pages.

One of her term assignments at the Sherwin School was the production of forty "character portraits," which meant pencil drawings in a more or less finished form, taken from life. There were several other pads at her apartment, filled with quick notes which she had made while she sat waiting in this very Navy sedan: cheerful young faces under white-topped caps, more weathered and responsible ones under the same caps heavy with gold braid; figures on the sidewalk; her own friends. This pad was scarcely begun.

The Graphic Arts instructor would accept most of these sketches once they were worked up, she thought. Her chief talent was the catching of a quick likeness. There was the one of Chester Verney, Anna Tannehill's recently acquired husband, the heavy good looks of his Roman-emperor face felicitously echoed in the dusty plaster cast which she had sketched behind his head. There were the two or three others she had done at that same party. And here were the two which she had flung down in twenty lines apiece, half an hour ago: the white-over-alled legs of a man, sprawling in an irresistibly comic attitude from behind a cement mixer that hid the rest of his body, and a more elaborate one. The latter had started out as an atmosphere sketch in the Doré manner—shafts of light falling from a high window across eerily shrouded forms—and had changed with the introduction of a figure, that of Lieutenant Coree standing on one leg, clasping the other shin in both hands, and looking agonized. Noel Bruce laughed aloud, looking at this souvenir. The lieutenant had been swearing under his breath, and you could almost see his lips move.

She gave a little start and closed the pad. Lieutenant Coree himself was standing beside the car. Noel's dark glance turned to him, her artist's eyes once more taking in every detail of his face. It was a long face, good-looking, tanned, hazel-eyed, with two heavy black bars of eyebrow that lent a humorous emphasis to his direct gaze. There was nothing ingenuous about it. Lieutenant Coree had seen all kinds, and could handle them, and had enough good humor left over to look like that.

His first remark was unexpected. "What are you doing now," he inquired, glancing at the sketch pad, " 'booking a delicious bit composed of a stone, a stump, and one mushroom?' "

Noel looked amazed and then grinned. "You're continually surprising me, Lieutenant Coree. How come you can quote *Little Women*, of all things?"

He gave her a sidelong and confidential look. "My sister and I had measles at the same time. I used to pretend to sneer when Mother read it aloud... However—" He became suddenly businesslike, gesturing toward the dock. "I got myself into a jam, in there. That ship lacks a radar part that has to be installed tonight—and the only one we can get hold of is out at Point Montara, which they tell me is a good way off."

"Not so bad," she said. "About thirty miles, down the Skyline Boulevard. It's a slow ride, but otherwise—"

"Here's the thing. You're working overtime already, aren't you? I'd better call the Twelfth Naval District and ask for another driver who's just come on."

"What is this," said Noel, "a dishonorable discharge? Your ticket said I was to take you wherever you wanted to go."

"Naturally I'd rather have you." He smiled at her. "And it would save time. Look, you must be hungry. Why don't we find a place— No? You mean you'll eat with nobody under the rank of commander?"

"Rear Admiral," Noel corrected him. "But I'd like to get your job done first."

"Nobly spoken," said the lieutenant approvingly. "And then—might we have dinner afterward? The Navy would owe you a bang-up meal by that time."

"I'd like that," she told him. The party she was supposed to be attending had vanished from her mind.

The drive to Point Montara took well over an hour, and long before they had reached the fork in the road which led to it, Noel was conscious that she had made a mistake in declining the chance to eat before she started. At least it must be that which was affecting her disposition, for to her surprise and shame she found herself trying to squabble with her passenger. He'd made some remark about having asked for the introduction to her at the Servicemen's Art Center. Since numerous other men had maneuvered for a meeting with her, she couldn't exactly be blamed for taking this as a personal compliment, but she felt foolishly annoyed when his next words gave it a different meaning: he had wanted to meet someone who knew the art school crowd, who could tell him about the places they frequented both for work and relaxation. Well, why not? She bit her lip in vexation at herself, and changed the subject to the scenery, which should have been safe; and five minutes later flared into a regular temper over some opinion he expressed. Miles Coree only looked amused and kind, and that made her crosser than ever. Something was certainly wrong with her, and she preferred to blame it on hunger.

She sat fuming outside the supply warehouse at the Point, and when he returned she had the car's rear door open. "Won't you ride in style this trip?" she invited. "I might snap your head off again if you were in the front seat."

He accepted this also with entire good humor, saying that if she didn't feel like talking he might try to sleep. He stretched his long frame slantwise across the rear seat and looked utterly relaxed. Noel started the car with a jerk.

The night was warm and mild, but an autumn fog muffled the western side of the peninsula. She drove steadily but cautiously, although on such a night the traffic on the Skyline was thin. The headlights of a car some distance behind kept illuminating the fog and then disappearing as her sedan rounded curve after curve. The rhythm was almost hypnotic: a straight stretch, and the fog milkily shining; a curve, and the return of darkness cut only by her own lights.

She became aware that the illumination behind her was steadier, that the car behind must have lessened the distance between them. She supposed it would be passing her, and she pulled to the side of the road.

It was not passing her. It was slowing as it came abreast of her car, edging over, pushing her deliberately toward the ditch. She fought to drop back, but there was no room. Her left hand gripped the wheel, her right automatically groped behind the seat for a wrench. She opened her lips, but the choked sound of warning and appeal was lost in a terrifying roar from the back seat.

Her passenger, bellowing imprecations, had flung open the rear door and was out on the road almost as soon as the car had stopped. He was heading for the other car; but its driver, after one quick look around, tramped on the gas pedal. The tail-light shot ahead, rounded a corner, disappeared.

"Get over!" Miles Coree grated, shoving Noel bodily from behind the wheel and flinging himself in. The engine was still going. It seemed as if he lifted the car out of the ditch by main strength, sending it flying forward in pursuit. "Trying to hold you up, were they?" he said in a grimly conversational tone. "We'll catch up with those gentlemen and point out their error." The car swung right and left, throwing her against the side. She managed to gasp, "No, please don't try. You don't know the road. It's no use!"

They wheeled around another curve, and he fought the steering gear, cursing under his breath. "Look," she cried, "the fog's thinner here—it's straight for half a mile, and we can't see a tail-light. They got away."

"I'm afraid you're right," said Lieutenant Coree, still grimly. The car slackened speed. "And what's more, I'm afraid this axle's bent."

"When I went into the ditch," she agreed, taking a shuddering breath.

He put on the brake at once, turning toward her. "That scared you, didn't it? I don't wonder. If you feel like crying, don't mind me."

"Thank you, but I don't. Not my style," said Noel, fighting to keep her voice level. She felt the man move close to her and link his arm firmly with hers, clasping her hand. His other hand settled over hers.

For several minutes neither of them spoke. She found her heartbeats settling to normal, her prickling skin smoothing out; and dimly she was aware that in the past quarter-hour she and the man beside her had passed from the beginning stage of friendship into a new sphere in which anything could happen.

She turned her head and looked at him, nodding swiftly. He released her hand and said, "All right now? You made a quick job of it. That's good going."

"The reaction got me for a minute," said Noel competently. "You won't mind if I take the wheel again? Then I'll be really over my scare."

A moment later, starting the car, she began to laugh. "If I was scared, it can't have been anything to the way those men must have felt! They thought I was alone, of course—and then to have you rise from the back seat with that quarter-deck bellow—!"

"Rather like old-style Chinese warfare, wasn't it?" said Coree cheerfully. "Make hideous faces and yell and try to frighten your enemy without firing a shot. Just the same, I'd like to get my hands on those characters."

"I wonder," said Noel, "if those ensigns on the sidewalk—you remember, when you came up with my ticket?—if they could have been talking about you. They were referring to somebody who could 'go off like a block-buster when so inclined.' Does this happen often, may I ask?"

"Certainly. The whole Fleet trembles when Coree merely steps aboard ship. And when it comes to active duty—well, you noticed that the war had stopped? But I don't much like that term 'block-buster.' Obsolete," said Miles Coree with a rueful shake of the head. "Don't you think, Miss Bruce, that—oh, the hell with this formality. Should you mind if I called you Noel?"

"Considering that you saved me from worse than death, or something, how could I mind?" She swung the car into Geary Boulevard.

"Worse than death. I suppose so, yes." Coree looked straight ahead, the street lights illuminating his dark face, which just now wore a puzzled expression. "There was something queer about that attempt at a hold-up. Did you catch a glimpse of the men in the car?"

"I didn't have a chance, what with trying to avoid a smash. Did you?"

"Not what you'd call a good look. There were two of them, one smallish, with his collar well up around his face, and the other—the driver—a bigger man. His collar was turned up, too, but I could see he had a heavy neck—looked as if he hadn't a neck at all, it was so thick… The license plate of the car had been carefully smeared with mud, did you notice?"

"I see what you mean about its being queer," said Noel slowly, "because I had the feeling that they'd followed us all the way out from town, and waited at that fork in the road near Montara, and then followed us back, choosing a place and time—as if it were this special car they were after, instead of any lone woman's. I don't know—is that a very secret radar part, Lieutenant Coree?"

"Make it Miles, will you?— The radar part doesn't signify. Those men, if you remember, didn't know I was in the car."

"Well, it's over. I suppose we'll never know." Noel was silent for a long time, until she drew up once more at the Fort Mason docks. Miles Coree also seemed to put the inexplicable adventure behind him; he completed his errand, returned to her, and was openly cheerful about the prospect of drinks and a late dinner. "I suppose you've got to turn in some sort of explanation with your car?" he inquired. "I'll do a signed statement as witness, got to preserve your reputation as a driver. Full speed ahead, sailor!"

San Francisco's curfew laws being what they are, there were only two hours left of the evening; but those two hours were plenty.

Noel knew pretty well what was happening to her, from their sudden mood of gaiety over dinner, from the way it felt to dance with Miles Coree, and the confidences that slipped out to the surprise of each. "I've never told that to anyone else," they kept saying, looking amazed. She kept reminding herself to go easy, that she didn't know anything about this long-faced man with the laughter in his eyes.

And yet, actually, by the end of the evening she did know a good deal about him. She knew that he'd studied at M. I. T. and meant to go back into communications work after the Navy released him. Its reluctance to do so, he said, was flattering but inconvenient. There was an uncle whom he described vaguely as having something to do with radio, who'd give him a job. He talked about his parents, with an affectionate softening of his face that made her realize, even more than his words, how close was his tie to them. He produced pictures; Noel's eyebrows went up at the unstudied glimpses of background, and the stamp of aristocracy on the faces of his father and mother. "Isn't she lovely?" she breathed over the last photograph. "Like a duchess. Was it taken after you went to sea? She looks so sad—"

"I'm afraid she was," Coree said, "but not over me. Here—I haven't shown you this one. That's my sister..."

He bent his head, considering, and added, "Rather a tragedy there." His voice stayed low and unemotional, but came intimately to her ears; the music and the deafening babble in the Cirque Room went far away as she sat close beside him at their small table. He said that there were only the most formal relations between his sister and the elder Corees; she had cut herself off by marrying someone who'd been involved in a rousing scandal. The sister believed he was innocent, and he may have been, but her parents' hearts were nearly broken by the marriage. If he'd been proved innocent—if the situation had meant only a quiet divorce—if he had been socially unsuitable but thoroughly respectable—in any of these circumstances they could have accepted it. As it was, she was lost to them. "My brothers and I see Kitty, of course," he added, "but Mother's feelings won't change."

Noel looked at him, her eyes dark with sympathy. He met the look and held it. "A nice girl, aren't you?" he said softly. His tone was light, but she'd never liked a compliment better.

A little after midnight he dismissed the cab at the mouth of the narrow street in which she lived. They stood in darkness at the foot of the steps that rose to the gray door of her gray lodging-house. He said, "You're fun to take out, Noel. This evening did something for my state of mind."

"Including the Chinese warfare?"

"That added a new flavor, though I shan't expect it on our next date." He put a finger under her chin and gently tilted up her face. "Do you ever?" he asked elliptically.

"Now and then, for an unusually nice man," she said, and laughed, and lifted her mouth to his.

It was the last carefree moment she was to know for a long, long time.

When they finally drew apart they gazed at each other in an almost comic consternation. "Did that really happen?" Miles Coree murmured, and tried it again. Whatever it was, it had really happened. Noel stood there in the half darkness and gazed mutely up at him, shaken and dazzled.

He said in a rather unsteady voice, "This—this calls for some thought. No, my lovely girl, don't move away. Stay here a minute. Damn it, I can't think, I'm dizzy—everything's changed."

She said faintly, "I knew it was coming, but I didn't know it would be like this."

He laid his cheek against her dark hair, rocking her gently to and fro. "Bless you, you darling," he said. "Here, can't we sit down on the steps and talk this over? What a place for discovering you've fallen in love. I should have kept that cab and bribed the driver to go away."

"Miles, I can't stay long. There's tomorrow—"

"Tomorrow! Hell, I can't even see you in the morning, I'm on duty! There are a few things I'd like to get straight. In the first place, are you spoken for, or anything?" She shook her head. "It'd be a bit ironic if I tried to move in on another fellow's territory. You see—I'd better tell you why I'm free as the air myself. My fiancée lived here in town, and it seems that while I was away she married somebody else."

A dozen remembered phrases rushed together and fused in Noel's mind. She turned in his encircling arm and gazed at him. "Miles, you don't by any chance mean Tannehill—Anna Tannehill?"

"Yes."

"But—she couldn't have done that to you."

"Seems she could."

"Not Anna! She's the loveliest—the kindest— Miles, I never knew that she was engaged to you, to anyone."

"No? Well, it's all over now. She is lovely, and kind. I've thought that perhaps it wasn't her fault. She had to wait a long time, though she seemed to think it was all right that I put off applying for discharge when I found my specialty was needed. The—man in the case may have taken advantage of that kindness of hers, knowing well enough that he was poaching. Not a nice trick," said Miles Coree softly.

Noel gave an involuntary gasp, and his grip on her shoulder slackened. She said in a whisper, "Miles, I—I have to—"

Down the narrow street footsteps sounded, wearily approaching the rooming house. She got to her feet swiftly. "That's Miss Ibsen, she lives on my floor. Oh, I must say good night. There will be time later, we have all the time there is, now."

"But not right away, worse luck!" He stood looking down at her, frowning. "Tomorrow there's some unfinished business I've got to do, and Friday morning I've got to take up my reservations or I'll miss seeing my family. I'll be back by the twenty-seventh at the latest, but—"

She said nervously, "We can talk then. We can write letters. I'll be right here, Miles."

The woman of the tired footsteps was nearly upon them. He said, "Good night, dear." Noel turned and almost ran up the steps, waiting at the top for her fellow lodger. She did not look back.

In silence the middle-aged woman and the young one mounted the inner flight of stairs. At the top, Miss Ibsen said testily, "That draft! Somebody's left the door to the back staircase open." She clumped down the hall to shut it, and then unlocked her own door and disappeared.

Noel went to her window and looked cautiously down.
Miles Coree was still on the sidewalk below; he tilted his head
up toward her lighted window, and touched his officer's cap.
She drew back and sat down, shivering. That's a nice beginning, she thought; I was too much of a coward to tell him that I
was the one who introduced Chester Verney to Tannehill, that
I fairly threw them at each other. Well, all right. I'll put it in a
letter. Maybe it won't mean anything to him, and maybe it will.
Might be I never will see him again, after all.

She felt absently in her pocket for that souvenir of the
early evening, the sketch pad topped with the portrait of
Chester Verney. It wasn't in her uniform pocket, and it hadn't
been on the seat of the car when she turned it in at the Twelfth
Naval District. Funny...Miles had noticed that drawing, and
had asked who was its subject. He didn't know Chester Verney
by sight, then.

Well, he would after he looked at that picture. She'd never
done better at catching a likeness. Where on earth had that
sketch pad gone?

She thought, Just forget it. Forget everything until he
comes back, on the twenty-seventh... She took off her coat
and blouse, and her brows drew together as she inspected the
bruise on her shoulder where Miles Coree's hand had gripped
it unconsciously. "Not a nice trick."

Forget it until the twenty-seventh.

On the afternoon of the twenty-first of September, Noel saw
the screaming headlines.

CHAPTER TWO

THE NEWSPAPERS, OF COURSE, played up the Bohemian angle of the case for all it was worth, and maybe more. Given as fantastic a crime as San Francisco had seen in years, they were not content. They saw fit to imply a background of attic studios lit by guttering candles; characters in velvet jackets and flowing ties; parties straight out of *Trilby* and Rudolph-and-Mimi relationships which outdid opera.

Like many journalistic implications, these were partly true and mostly a long way from accuracy. A few of the persons involved were cheerfully amoral, to be sure, but not one of them would have been caught dead in a flowing tie—witness Papa Gene Fenmer, whose full-dress elegance at the Sherwin Art School soirées fairly dazzled the beholders. It was a far cry from a candlelit attic to Anna Tannehill's apartment on Post Street, though it was called a studio and housed some of her smaller works of sculpture. There was Rita Steffany, of course, and there was Will Rome. Those two lived up to some of the tradition. On the other hand, consider Daisy Watkins (sculpture) who never went any place unless escorted by her cousin Paul Watkins (ceramics); consider Noel Bruce (line drawing), who earned her living and tuition fees and did hours of class work besides, leaving no time at all for orgies.

Also, scarcely any of the action took place either at the School or in the studios. This was a nasty blow for the reporters, who had to compensate by stressing the drama of contrast. You know the sort of thing. Utilitarian background, no more colorful than a factory—artists working so hard and seriously that you could hardly distinguish them from the laborers casting cement fixtures in the next room—and then, in the midst of all this, the grisly discovery, the sudden intrusion of a corpse from high life into the Plaster Works. There was drama, indeed, but what wouldn't they have given for a few fishnet draperies in the old Bohemian style!

There are several Plaster Works in San Francisco, and at more than one of them sculptors have taken over a portion of floor space for work on their larger models and sculptures in stone. This one was near North Beach, not far from the Sherwin School, and so placed between two obscure cross-streets that it occupied nearly a solid chunk in the middle of a block. It was a great warehouse of a place, the exterior weather-beaten and ramshackle, with a gray wooden fence enclosing a small paved courtyard; the interior divided into two unequal portions by a dingy wooden partition six or seven feet high, with a second-hand door hung crazily in its single opening. One entered the building by a broad entrance where trucks could drive in, by a smaller door from an alley at the opposite end, or by a door from the courtyard.

In the larger space there were high windows. Their glass was none too clean, and their warped frames let in thin streams of air. The whole place had the chill and drafty feeling of an old barn, and added to it was the dank smell of cement, damp plaster, wet clay. White dust had been ground and grimed into the floor for years, and under the long tables with their marble slabs for casting were corners which held hardened deposits of dirt. Besides these tables, the chief article of furniture was a cement mixer. The decor consisted of an unending frieze, just below the windows, of plaster casts furred with the dust of twenty years.

Behind the wooden partition, in the smaller portion of the Works, were the same high windows—here somewhat cleaner—and the same frieze of casts. Here, however, the foot trod upon heavy clay that smeared thin, dried, and powdered into countless footprints. There were sacks of it propped against the walls, and some wooden boxes lined with metal that held still more. Tools, pipe, great folded squares of dingy cloth, were placed and stacked in a purposeful confusion. Dominant, catching the eye as a figure or nearly human shape will do in any composition, were the three large statues in progress of work. When these were swathed in their protective cerements of wet cloth, the scene was far from glamorous to uninitiated eyes.

Naturally the sculptors and their friends saw something different: their place of work, comfortless but alive with creation. The hideous long-bodied stove could be coaxed to a cheering heat for thawing numbed fingers and making coffee on cold days, and the fact that its counterpart in the mold-making section was used for cooking up countless batches of malodorous glue had ceased to bother anyone. As for the masses of clay in work, no matter how formless a stage they might be in, the sculptors saw life in them.

On September 21st, at half-past one in the afternoon, Eugene Fenmer paid his regular visit of instruction to his students at the Plaster Works. He left his car outside the wooden fence and marched through the courtyard with a dignity nowise impaired by the voluminous white overall suit he was wearing. His was the complexion of Santa Claus and the expression of G. B. Shaw, with some length and shagginess subtracted from the white beard and mustache. Papa Gene's elegance was as much a part of him as his overwhelming vigor, a combination that made his reputation with young women easy to understand.

"Afternoon, Rome!" he bellowed cheerfully to the man working in the courtyard, and as he went by cast a swift appraising glance at the shape emerging from Rome's block of stone. Will Rome was an independent sculptor, not one of the Sherwin students, and old Fenmer's eyes expressed the respect of one artist for another.

Rome only looked up and nodded in acknowledgment of the greeting, but after Fenmer had disappeared inside the building, he laid down his hammer in order to light a cigarette. He stood smoking it in quick deep drags; once he looked as if idly at the open windows of the sculptor's section. This season was high summer in San Francisco, and Rome wiped sweat from his forehead, with the same gesture pushing back a shock of unkempt dark hair. His full mouth moved slightly as if he were talking to himself; he flung down the cigarette, took a deep breath of the sun-heated air, and once more bent his melancholy eyes upon his work.

Inside the building, Eugene Fenmer had completed his march through the plaster-casting section and his affable words and nods to the workmen, had gone through the door in the wooden partition and had made his ceremonious entry into his students' workroom. His dark gaze traveled swiftly about the space, noting the two uncovered clay models and the third one still swathed in wet rags with an additional covering of oilcloth. Then his white eyebrows flew up and he sniffed mightily.

"God, what a stink!" Papa Gene shouted. "Who's been here, the Art Critics' Association?"

There was appreciative laughter from the three students in the room, echoed by subdued snickers from the plaster casters outside.

"It's that damned glue, Papa Gene," Rita Steffany said in an annoyed drawl, low-pitched. "They've had it on to cook every day this week, and I'll swear they've forgotten it at night and let it boil dry."

"So? It must be a new brand. Haven't you complained?"

Steffany shrugged. "Necessary evil, we figured." She was an arresting young woman, white of skin and shining black of hair, with a sensuous curled mouth lipsticked a deep crimson. Her long black eyes slid sideward at the instructor as she spoke, as if she could not even discuss boiling glue without a suggestion of sex.

Fenmer nodded, dismissing the subject. "Let's get to work," he said, and turned to one of the uncovered clay models.

It represented a young flyer striding forward—presumably toward his airplane—with uplifted face and a dedicated expression. To the lay eye it appeared conventional in conception and somewhat hesitant in execution. How it looked to Fenmer was apparent more in his omissions than in his words.

He remarked kindly enough, "Well, Watkins, you're getting along with it," and went on to point out some technical faults; few enough, one would think, but when he had finished and turned away, Daisy Watkins' face was red and she bit her lip as if to keep back tears. She stood beside her statue with her angular body drooping in relaxation after this weekly ordeal, but her gray eyes were disappointed. Each week it seemed as if she hoped, against all the honest dictates of her training, that genius had magically visited her; each week Papa Gene praised with faint damns, and visibly she acknowledged his justice.

She threw a quick glance at the young man who sat in a corner, well out of the sculptors' way, in a position where he could rest his head against an angle of the wall. This was her cousin, Paul Watkins, a Sherwin student but not one of the sculptors. His presence here in the afternoons had become habitual. He sat watching, saying little or nothing, hardly moving except for his fingers which absently kneaded a heavy ball of clay. He was not looking at Daisy now. He gazed straight before him, his head and neck stiffly held.

Fenmer said nothing for a moment, while he scrutinized Rita Steffany's model of a soldier crouching to talk to a small child which leaned against his knee. Steffany braced herself, but wore a look of confidence; when Papa Gene really criticized one took it as an honor, at the same time wishing he did not have to bellow in competition with the cement mixer beyond the partition. He was outdoing himself today. He raved, called on all three members of the Trinity, and thought up some surprising ways to describe her modeling of the baby's cheek and the soldier's thigh. Then he came to a dead stop, took an immaculate handkerchief from his overalls pocket, and wiped his heated brow. Then he beamed suddenly at the students.

"Well," he said, "quick enough work with only two of you to take apart. Not enough to keep the old man busy."

"It's hardly our fault, Papa Gene," Daisy Watkins said in her pleasant voice, "Tannehill walking out on us the way she did. You could have spent a full hour with her!"

"Ah, Tannehill!" Fenmer heaved a mock sigh. "That gorgeous wench! Still honeymooning, I suppose?"

"Nobody's heard any different," Steffany drawled.

Papa Gene turned to the shrouded statue, lifted the oilcloth cover and tested the dampness of the covering rags. "Better wet her down," he said, and began deftly to lift off the cloths. "Our bride ought to be back some day soon, when her hand heals up. If she lets that Verney character she married keep her away from this piece of work, I'll strangle her personally. Him too."

"You think she has a good chance in the memorial competition?" Watkins asked.

"How do I know what those idiots of judges are going to think?" Fenmer roared. "She's done a damn' good job, though, and I'd be a fool myself if I didn't recognize it." He went on working, whistling softly, and the two women sat down on boxes and lit cigarettes. Summer air drifted through the high windows, wafting to and fro the disagreeable odor which Steffany had diagnosed as glue. The cement mixer clanked and ground, clanked more slowly, and stopped so that in the comparative silence the sound of hammer and chisel came loud and rapid from the courtyard.

Fenmer's whistled tune trailed off into incoherence; he paused in his task, looking puzzled. "I thought Tannehill had got farther than this?" he said in a tone of unusual mildness.

The torso of the third statue was uncovered. Its clay seemed to be roughly streaked and lumpy; Fenmer began to lift off the cloths which covered the rest of the figure.

The students had been murmuring to each other, paying little attention to the unveiling. They had seen this piece of work from its inception, and had frankly admired and envied it, so that it was as familiar to them as their own models. It was called "Woman at the Grave"—sentimental enough, as Anna Tannehill herself admitted, but lifted far above banality by its power and certainty. The figure of the Woman was sprawled prone in the terrible awkwardness of unself-conscious grief, the head lifted slightly to rest on a low mound.

Yet now, as they looked at the model with sudden attention, there was something odd about it: as if the artist, dissatisfied with the surface modeling, had torn down most of her work and begun again.

"But that's not—" Steffany said, startled into vagueness. "That doesn't look like—she hasn't worked on it for about two weeks, but it couldn't have dried in that time?"

"It isn't dry," said Eugene Fenmer. There was electricity in his voice now. "There's been some mischief." He turned an awe-inspiring glare on the three students. "Did anyone—no, I can't believe that one of you would have touched or uncovered another's model?"

"Certainly not!" Steffany got up, her black brows knitted, and moved for a closer look at the clay torso. Daisy Watkins was doing an extremely slow take, sitting still with her mouth slightly open.

No longer working with delicacy, Fenmer took the cloths from the statue's head. "Good God," he said, "what's this supposed to be, collage? There's hair—"

Watkins, finally aroused, stood up and craned. "It's got— *shoes* on!" she said in a loud unnatural voice, and drew in her breath with the effect of a shriek.

For an instant nobody moved; there was no sound in the room, for outside in the courtyard the chipping noises had abruptly ceased. Then Eugene Fenmer stepped back hurriedly, swung toward the partition, and in a voice that seemed to rattle the plaster casts on the wall, shouted "Beef!" It was the traditional cry for help in moving heavy objects.

A husky workman enveloped in grimy white overalls came through the door. "Whatcha want done, Mr. Fenmer?" he said casually. "Can the two of us do it, or d'ya want Mike too?"

Fenmer looked down at his hands, as if surprised to find them shaking. "Yes, yes—get Mike. And bring a lever."

"A lever?" the workman began, when the door opened abruptly and Will Rome walked in, wiping stone-dust from his hot face with a sleeve. "Something up?" his deep voice asked casually; his eyes, sad-shaped like a hound's, moved from one to another of the students. "What's got shoes on, Watkins?"

"Don't know," Fenmer answered for her. "It may be a practical joke, or vandalism, but I—here, Rome, you'll do to help." He moistened dry lips and jerked his head toward the stolid workman, returning with the lever. "I—I want to look under Tannehill's statue."

"Under it?" Rome said uncomprehendingly; but he bent his big frame to assist. Fenmer squatted on his heels and peered under the shell of clay.

"Let it down," he said in a stifled voice, rising hastily. "There's a—a dead body there."

Again, for the space of seconds, nobody moved. Rome stayed where he was, gazing up over his shoulder at Fenmer, his heavy face slack and pale with horror. The workman named Mike, standing idly by, let out his breath as if he had been struck in the stomach.

Then Paul Watkins slid carefully from his stool. "Daisy and Rita," he said crisply, "get out of here!"

His cousin glared wildly around at him, clapped a hand to her mouth and bolted for the courtyard. Rita Steffany followed her, pale and wide-eyed, but alert. In the silence the men could hear her feet outside. She began to run purposefully as soon as the door closed behind her.

Paul said, "Mike, shut the partition door, will you?" The faces of the plaster workmen staring through were abruptly pushed back, and the dingy panels cut them off from sight but not from hearing. "Papa Gene," the young man went on in a low voice, "there's no doubt, I suppose?"

Fenmer's neat white head moved from side to side.

Paul went with his odd stiff-necked gait toward the grisly exhibit and bent over it. "We thought it was the glue," he said, with a wry smile that sat oddly on his young face. While the others watched him dully, he pulled aside the oilcloth which Fenmer had dropped over the head of the statue.

Upon the low mound on which the Woman's head rested a thin layer of clay had been smoothed, and faintly scratched on it as if on a flat gravestone were four words and two dates. There was a sound of harsh breathing as the men leaned forward; one of the workmen said, "What the hell—" in a muffled voice; Will Rome cleared his throat and read aloud slowly, "Claude Pruitt, 1903-1943."

He shook his untidy head as if he were dizzy. "But if this is—if somebody called Claude Pruitt's been stuck into Anna's model, God knows why—it can't be, Fenmer! This is 1946!"

One of the craziest things about the whole set-up, Red Hobart later pointed out to his colleagues on the San Francisco *Eagle*, was the way this Paul Watkins took command and the others let him get away with it—that queer fish with his immature-looking face, like a college sophomore before the war; with his old-maidish concern about his own health, and that uncanny habit of sitting still and letting his eyes follow you around. Sure, he'd had a commission in the Army, but he hadn't been a lieutenant for more than a few months before he was thrown out of that jeep at Camp Edwards and brought in for dead with a broken neck... Maybe he was just too dumb to take in the horror.

Red, in his capacity as reporter, had arrived at the Plaster Works a good five minutes before the police. It was Rita Steffany who'd tipped him off—gone straight across the courtyard to the little office and telephoned. Nothing like a girl friend on the scene of the crime! She had managed to slip him a few extra details before the cops arrived and threw everybody out of the sculptors' workroom. Some beat, hey boys?

Thus Red in the *Eagle*'s city room, on his return from the scene of the crime: a blond young-old man, his eyeballs veined with tiny red threads, his voice rough from smoking but indomitably cocky: his face as knobbily round and his manner as brash as those of the comedian Red Skelton, to which resemblance he owed his nickname. "What a yarn, what a yarn!" Red exclaimed, casting himself down at his typewriter desk. "And what'll you bet those so-and-sos in the office pull me off it? They've got a down on me—"

He proved a true prophet. When the corpse turns out to be somebody against whom a reporter has violent prejudices, the editors generally choose someone with a more open mind to cover the story.

Paul Watkins had called the Homicide Division from the small glass-enclosed office at the far side of the courtyard. He had also, after a minute's thought, put in another call during which he spoke low and soothingly. It was not a long conversation, but he had scarcely finished it and returned to the awed and unsteady group in the mold-making section when the police came. The tall, grizzled man with the mournful Irish face, Inspector Geraghty, went through the preliminary routine with a speed which attested to his long experience on the force. Then there was a wait, while muffled voices and sounds and flashes of light came from behind the board partition; a long, nerve-racking twenty minutes or so. The sculptors sat without a word, and consumed cigarettes; Daisy Watkins kept gulping nervously; Eugene Fenmer's Santa Claus cheeks had faded to a mottled mauve.

When the tall man came through the partition he was looking grim and more elderly than when he had gone in. He said, "Any of you know Chester Verney personally?"

His eye happened to catch that of the plaster-works foreman. The man coughed; he said nervously, "Jeez, Inspector, you mean the big-time mouthpiece?" The remark, however, was drowned out by a horrified babble from the artists.

Geraghty waited until it died down. "You all did?" he said thoughtfully. "It was this group he went around with, then? H'm."

"Inspector," said Fenmer in a shadow of his usual great voice, "that isn't—that body in there—" His white head trembled.

"The body has not been identified. It will take some identifying," he added without inflection.

"But—your question, Inspector."

"I think I may tell you," said Geraghty, "that under the body there was a wallet which seems to be Chester Verney's property. Had his identification cards in it, and a wad of money."

"Under the body," Rita Steffany repeated faintly.

"Also, the corpse was—" Geraghty cleared his throat. "Was wearing a belt with an initialed buckle."

"Wearing a—"

"A belt. Nothing else except shoes." He went on, impervious to the looks of sick horror on the faces of artists and workmen, "We've been in touch with Mr. Verney's office and we find he hasn't been in town for a couple of weeks, not since his marriage was announced. If this body isn't his, it's something of a coincidence that his wallet should be—hidden with it, and that the initials on the buckle are the same as his. I don't think we'll be wasting time if I ask you a few questions about your connection with Verney. You first, please, Mr. Fenmer."

"Wait, please, Inspector," Papa Gene said. "This is almost a community proceeding. Not for our friends the plaster casters, naturally, but for the rest of us. If you're going to ask us all when we last saw him—I believe that's one of the stock questions?—I can almost answer for my students here, and Mr. Rome. We were all together in the workroom here"—he gestured toward the partition—"along with one or two other guests, Hobart from the *Eagle* and a young girl named Noel Bruce, another Sherwin student. I can tell you the date: Saturday, September the eighth. It was," said Papa Gene, rising and moving toward the detective with his hands thrust into his overall pockets, "on the occasion when Verney's marriage was announced. His bride arranged the party—Anna Tannehill, one of my students."

"Oh, my God," Daisy Watkins said as if talking to herself, "Tannehill's statue. No, that's too horrible! Not Verney, not her own—"

"Cut it, Watkins," Will Rome broke in. His voice sounded surly. "Everyone's thought of that."

"Maybe you'd enlighten me, Mr. Rome," said Geraghty dryly.

Rome had not taken his eyes from the inspector's face since the questions had begun. "Anna Tannehill was working on that clay model, up to about four days before that party Fenmer mentioned." He spoke rapidly, sounding hoarse. "She hasn't been here since, except to the party. Somebody—if that's Verney, somebody tore down her work and—"

"I see." The inspector's head turned toward the partition for a long look. None of these revelations seemed to startle him. "His own wife's statue, h'm?" He turned back briskly. "Now I think I've got the general idea. There'll be a few questions, as I said, and we—"

The door to the courtyard opened and hastily shut after admitting a plainclothes officer. For the moment when it stood open, the crowd of reporters waiting outside surged forward, straining for a look at the silent group within. As the officer finished his low-toned remarks to Geraghty, a woman's voice was clearly audible in the yard. "But I belong in there!" it said. "Please, won't you take me to the person in charge?"

"That's Tannehill," Will Rome said sharply.

Geraghty glanced at him. "Somebody must have let her know what happened," he said mildly. "You, Mr. Rome?"

"I did," Paul Watkins said, clearing his throat. "I—of course I couldn't know who—I called her up. You see, I knew where she was, and it—well, Inspector, it was her clay model that—"

"I see, Mr. Watkins. That's enough." Paul fell silent, dropping his eyes to the ball of clay he was still mechanically kneading. The inspector added, "Saves time, maybe. Just the same, I'd rather not have had her come here. Okay, Kotock, I guess you can let her in."

The plainclothes man opened the door again. From the murmuring voices of the newsmen Hobart's cocky tones rang out: "Good girl, Tannehill! But how's about an exclusive for me?"

"Exclusive? Don't be silly, Hobart," the woman entering the Plaster Works called over her shoulder. "If I have to give an interview, it's for all of you."

She faced about, blinking at the westering sun which shone through the dingy windows, nursing a bandaged left hand against the breast of a thin dark coat. Her gray-blue eyes, widely set under a serene forehead, went from the silent and uneasy group of workmen to the haggard faces of her friends. Then, with a turn of the head that brought out the beautiful modeling of her chin and throat, she looked at Geraghty. "You're the police captain?" she said in a gentle voice.

"Inspector. Geraghty's my name. You're Mrs. Chester Verney?"

Anna Verney inclined her head, the expression of puzzled awe still in her eyes. Her smooth blonde hair, upswept, seemed to catch and hold the light as she stood poised for another moment against the dull background; then she moved forward with effortless grace. The inspector looked at her gravely, as if weighing what he should say to her.

"I heard that there had been a—a dreadfully tragic discovery. Is it true, Inspector?" she said.

"Yes, it's true, Mrs. Verney."

"A man, dead, in my clay model?" Geraghty nodded, his shrewd look still taking her measure. Anna Verney smiled at him uncertainly. "I suppose you know," she said, "that I haven't touched it for nearly three weeks. I burned my hand"—she gestured toward the thick bandages—"and then I went away for a few days, so I—of course I know nothing about it. But I felt I must come."

"Where were you staying, Mrs. Verney? Mr. Watkins said he 'knew where to find you.' "

"I wasn't at home, that is, in my own studio. I was at my aunt's home in St. Francis Wood."

"With your aunt?"

"No. The housekeeper is there, no one else."

"Your husband wasn't with you, then."

"No. He's not in town."

"Oh? How long ago did he leave?"

The golden girl took her eyes from his face momentarily, and glanced at the motionless group of sculptors. She smiled at them, an alluring flash of vermilion and white. "About ten days ago. My friends there will tease the life out of me, Inspector, because we were supposed to be on a honeymoon! But—you were wrong after all, Papa Gene." She glanced at Fenmer, whose dark eyes came up to meet hers with a spark of something like warning. "Both Chet and I had our own way! We're civilized, after all."

Daisy Watkins had been sitting close to her cousin, gazing pallidly at Anna Verney and the inspector. Now, as if galvanized into involuntary speech, she said loudly, "Chet's in your statue! It's Ch—" and broke off with a strangled gasp as the police guard sprang forward and Geraghty swung round toward her.

Anna Verney had understood. Her face flushed a deep sudden crimson and as suddenly went white. She recoiled a step, looking piteously at the inspector.

"I'm sorry, Mrs. Verney," said Geraghty in a swift low voice. "Sit down over here, will you please? I couldn't foresee—" He turned back to the group, palpably controlling himself. "The rest of you," he said, "had better go down to headquarters and wait there, till I can talk to you. We can bring you back if it's necessary.—Yes, just as you are, Miss Steffany, nobody minds if you're in working clothes.—Got statements from the plaster casters, Kotock? Okay. They can go home. We'll keep in touch with them."

He waited until the two groups had dissolved, until the sound of their feet had died away through the courtyard gate. The voices of the reporters sounded like an embodied stage direction: "Mob mutters offstage." They were getting out of hand, waiting in the hot courtyard, seeing the witnesses rushed past them to the police cars.

Geraghty watched through one of the high windows—he was tall enough to see over the sill—until they had quieted down again. He looked twice at a round-faced young man who was leaning against the fence and chewing gum in a slow comfortable rhythm. "Lockett, by all that's holy," he told himself, silently chuckling. "Standing outside like a good little boy."

He turned back to the barnlike room, empty now except for the woman sitting with bowed head on the rickety stool in a corner. He spoke with the sympathetic courtesy that was one of his greatest assets.

"This has been a shock for you, Mrs. Verney, and perhaps an unnecessary one. We haven't made any positive identification. But—if you feel strong enough to talk to me a few minutes…?"

"Yes, I'm strong enough," said Anna Verney quietly.